# BEAUTIFUL
# SINNER

*USA TODAY* BESTSELLING AUTHOR

# SARA CATE

Cover design: Opulent Swag & Designs

*For the Patron Saint*

Dear reader,

The story you're about to read is about forbidden love. And what is more forbidden than a priest who finds himself torn between his vows and his sins in the face of love and passion? If you are sensitive to blasphemy and tested faith, you might find yourself offended by the vows he breaks. So be warned. He breaks them. A lot.

Enjoy.

Scan to listen to the
Beautiful Sinner playerlist

*"My kingdom for a kiss upon her
shoulder."*
*-Jeff Buckley*

# Chapter 1

## Cadence

Clint has dark curls on the top of his head and a smile that wins elections. And right now, he's aiming those million dollar ivories directly at me. Under his glowing stare, I see a story we could tell our grandkids, set to a picturesque film reel of European settings.

We met in Amsterdam, one of fifty on a bus tour with a horde of young Americans. We had our first kiss in Paris the day before he snuck his hand up my dress in the Chunnel on our way to London. Shortly after I went down on him in a red phone booth, we decided to leave the tour that brought us here from Los Angeles. We stayed with the group on the ferry that brought us to the Emerald Isle, but then it was just Clint, me, and a group of his closest friends. A couple guys and girls with smiles as bright as his.

"We're going rogue," he announces as we huddle into the cramped rental car I covered with my stressed out credit card and take off across the Irish landscape in search of absolutely nothing but feeling on top of the world. It's only been four days since we met, and already I see our wedding, magazine-worthy with a line of bridesmaids and his best friends in a lush green garden where he'll break down in brave tears when it comes time to say his vows to me. He'll talk about this day, our first day on our own, hands linked across the center console of this Opel Astra.

Every few moments he looks over with that twinkle in his eye, and I know that I've found it. I found what my sister has, and this time it's real.

"Babe, you're going to love this place. It's known for the music, and not like Coachella music either, babe. Like real traditional artists, you know. The authentic shit."

"I can't wait." I gleam toward him.

There's not a hint of fear in my heart when I'm with him. I don't care that I just forfeited my seat on the plane back to California or that I barely know him. When you know, you know. And every single thing in this past week has been practically transcendental.

I want to tell him I love him, and I know that's insane, but it's insane to let a moment like this pass.

One of the girls from the back leans forward to tap Clint on the arm to show him something on her phone. She has it aimed so it's out of my view, but not intention-ally. He laughs, and I look out the window so she doesn't feel awkward for not showing me.

It's past nine when we finally pull into a small town, and the sun has already set, leaving the area in darkness so that the only thing I make out when we drive in is a grand house with three floors and a large porch. It's beautiful.

It's so quiet when we get out of the car that I can hear distant waves rolling from out of the darkness. Clint waits at the front of the car for me and takes my hand so we can go in together. At the top of the porch is a sign on the wall: *Ennis Beach Bed & Breakfast*

It's quiet inside but brightly lit. There are voices coming from a room in the back, and one of the girls we're with shouts a loud "yoo-hoo" at which point the chatter in the back stops.

"Bloody hell," a gruff voice mutters as the ominous stomping comes nearer until a tall man in all black walks into the lobby. He looks annoyed with us, and I quickly avert my eyes, hoping he doesn't think it was me that so rudely called them up. Behind him, a young woman brushes past and rushes to the desk.

"Good evening," she says in a sing-song chime as she takes her place behind the desk. "Welcome to Ennis Beach."

"We're checking in," Clint says sweetly. "Last name, Thorn." He sends me a wink, and there's something about him saying my name that makes my insides flutter.

"Ah yes," the woman answers softly as she starts typing on the computer.

The tall man is still standing in the doorway, his eyes surveying us. I make myself busy by looking around the room, noticing that the house looks very much like a regular house, with old timey pictures along the wall. If it wasn't for the tall counter and computer and a stand with pamphlets in the entryway, you wouldn't even know this was a hotel—or technically a bed and breakfast as the door said.

I step away from Clint for a moment to stare at the pictures, noticing one with a stone gray church in front of a grassy field. The young couple standing in front makes me feel the warmth of romance, and a smile creeps onto my face.

Feeling eyes on me, I turn toward the doorway to the

dining room and notice the tall man is now watching me. His brow is curved slightly inward, creating a deep crease down the center of his forehead as he leans against the wide doorway, arms crossed.

"Americans?" he asks with his thick Irish accent.

"Yes, sir," Clint answers proudly.

"I'll need a credit card for the account," the woman says with a courteous smile.

Clint pats his pockets. "My wallet's in the car. You're not charging it yet, are you?"

"No. We just need one on file. You pay when you check out."

"Babe, would you mind?"

I almost get lost in the dimples in his cheeks that it takes me a moment to catch up to his question. "Oh, of course." Quickly, I open my purse and pull out my poor, battered AmEx to pass it to the woman. Clint pulls me against his body and places a kiss against my temple. The low hum he makes when he kisses me sends electricity down my spine.

"Okay, you're all booked for two rooms. They're both on the second floor. Rooms 201 and 202."

"This one is ours," Clint says as he takes one of the keys and pulls me toward the stairs. I let out a laugh as he pinches my ass. We rush up the stairs together, leaving the rest of his friends to sleep in the second room. I couldn't care less. This is our first real night alone in a hotel room. Right now, all I care about is him. I am living for only him.

Once we're alone in the room, Clint is fast to kiss me. He pulls my face up to his and his mouth hungrily devours mine.

"Oh baby, I can't get enough of you," he moans into my neck as he pulls up my dress, his fingers yanking my underwear aside. It's all happening so fast, I can barely breathe.

As he pushes me down into the bed, pressing himself between my legs, I want to pinch myself. I'm no idiot. I know our days won't always be this perfect, and there will be trials in our future, but with a start this passionate, I know there is no chance that it will ever completely fizzle out. Clint and I connect on another level.

The passion between us is so intense that it doesn't take him more than a few pumps inside of me before he's coming, jolting between my legs. In terms of reaching an orgasm myself, I guess it would have been nice if the passion fizzled out a little...just enough to give me a chance.

He pulls back and kisses my nose. "Sorry, baby. You just do something crazy to me."

I love that southern accent of his, so I smile and kiss him back. I'll take care of myself in the shower later.

"Come on, beautiful. We're going to the pub down the street." He climbs off of me and pulls his pants up.

"Okay," I answer with a forced smile. In truth, I'm exhausted. Today was exhilarating, but I just need time to slow down for a second.

"You'll come with us, right?" He leans down and kisses the top of my head.

"Of course," I answer sleepily.

The pub is lively, enough to wake me up from my sleepy haze after that quick romp with Clint in the hotel room. It's not at all what I expected. We've been to clubs and bars on this trip, but this is something else. It's a small space, full of people without feeling crowded. There is music coming from the other side of the pub, but as we squeeze through, Clint finds us a table and tells me to sit while he gets me a drink. Sitting alone, I look around at the crowd, noticing that it literally ranges from children to elderly. The table behind us has a carseat carrier in the booth with a baby fast asleep, no matter that it's loud as hell in here.

Leaning back, I see the music is coming from one of the tables squeezed in the corner. The musicians sit around the beer-soaked table with their instruments in their laps. Something about it makes me so happy that I'm glad I came out tonight.

A pair of bright green eyes catch my attention while I'm looking around, and I notice the man from the hotel is sitting at the bar with a pint of dark beer in his hands as he stares at me. That blank expression is still plastered on his face, and I send him an awkward smile and wave.

I don't have the guts to just stare at him the way he's staring at me, but as my eyes skim over him again, I realize that he's probably in his late thirties and a lot better looking than I noticed at first. Those round cheeks and full lips probably get all the ladies for him, but he's a little too rugged for me. His clothes look worn with a layer of dust over his black pants.

When he catches me staring again, he nods at me, and I quickly look away. Thankfully, Clint and his friends return in the next moment with the drinks, and I have to force down my dark beer.

The rest of the night turns into a blur. I blame the exhaustion and excitement from the day.

After one round, we're up dancing with the locals.

After two rounds, the room is spinning.

After three rounds, Clint is helping me as I stumble down the cobblestone road toward the hotel. I don't remember getting to the room or taking my clothes off because as soon as we started up the stairs, everything went black.

# Chapter 2

## Cadence

**W**ater.

It's the first thought in my head when the blinding sun beaming through the large windows wakes me from my twenty-feet-under sleep. Why is waking up with a hangover so abrupt? It's like being shot out of a canon and landing in an active volcano.

I need water.

Opening my eyes, I try to replay the events of the evening. I don't know how I ended up so drunk. I don't even remember drinking that much.

"Clint," I croak, reaching for him without moving my head. I'm afraid if I move at all, it will just split in two. The other side of the bed is empty. He must be in the shower or down at breakfast already.

He came back to the room with me last night. Didn't he? I remember him having to help me down the street because my wobbly legs couldn't fight the gravity that wanted to pull me onto the cobblestone ground.

God, I hope I didn't make too much of an ass of myself. I have a way of getting a little too friendly when I'm drunk. I do remember dancing with him, kissing him by the bar, resting my head on his shoulder in the booth. I'm still dressed, so I doubt we did it when we got back.

After a long waking process, I finally peel my body off the bed and look for any sign of Clint. Glancing around the cozy room with its ornate furniture and cozy armchair in the corner, I search for literally anything that belongs to me or Clint. We left our bags in the car last night before we went out. I figured we'd just get it all when we got back.

Maybe he's bringing it up now.

I need my phone. I don't know why, but I just want to check it. But I don't see my purse either. Fuck. Did I leave it at the pub? I wouldn't be surprised, although I've never managed to do that before.

God dammit, Clint. Where are you?

Convinced a shower will help make me feel normal, I climb out of bed, but first I stop at the window to look for Clint outside. Peeling the curtain back, I let out a gasp and not just because it's so bright it feels like knives in my skull, but I'm finally seeing what I missed last night when it was too dark to see the landscape around the hotel. The front of the building faces a broad, long beach. But it's not like the beaches I'm used to in California. The beach is vast, stretched far from the water to the shore, like a glistening floor of heavy dark sand that shimmers like glass.

Just to the right of the hotel, I can make out the parking lot where we parked the car. Now there are only two cars sitting out there, and neither of them is our red rental.

Heat crawls up my spine as I stare at the spot where our car used to be.

Where did they go? Without me.

That would be so strange for them to go somewhere without even waking me up. Maybe he tried, and I just drank too much. They're probably out sightseeing or getting something they need.

I force myself into the shower, but I can barely focus on the task of washing my body. My mind won't stop running through possibilities that don't result in something terrible.

But it still hurts that Clint would leave me behind. He's probably just downstairs, and I'm being dramatic.

It dawns on me as I get out of the shower that I don't have my bag, so I don't have clean clothes. I'm forced to put back on my dress that smells like the pub. It makes me sick pulling it onto my body—degrading and disgusting— like how I feel.

Slipping my sandals on, I walk next door and knock on the door Clint's friends slept in. There's no answer, so I go downstairs and the silence makes me nervous. Where is everybody?

The house is exquisite, but I can't enjoy that right now. Opposite the dining room, there is a sitting room with floor to ceiling windows that face the ocean. It's full of dark wood and plush rugs, old looking decorations but clean and fresh smelling.

I find myself staring out at the ocean because it is literally all I have at this point.

"You missed breakfast." A deep voice cuts through the silence. Spinning on my heels, I stare at the tall man from last night. Seeing his face suddenly brings back a flash of memory from the pub.

He was there. I remember him staring at me like he is right now. Like he doesn't approve of me, and right now, I'm not in the mood for it.

"I don't care," I grumble. The thought of breakfast turns my stomach anyway.

"Would you like some coffee?"

God, that sounds good. I hate to admit it. "Yes, please."

He turns away, and I notice he's dressed in black again. Black slacks with a matching button-up long-sleeve shirt with the sleeves rolled up to his elbows. I find myself staring at his backside as he pours a cup of coffee from the tall silver machine. He really fills out those pants nicely, and I immediately feel guilt for thinking that. I should be thinking about Clint and worrying that he's not hurt somewhere.

"Do you happen to know where my friends are?" I ask as he brings me a steaming cup with a handful of creamers and sugar packets.

"Have a seat," he says flatly, placing the coffee on the round coffee table between two oversized arm chairs.

"Okay," I reply with curiosity, dropping into the large chair. Something about this man is unsettling. The kind woman is nowhere in sight. It's literally just us in this house.

"Your friends are gone."

"I know," I answer as I pour two packets of sugar in my coffee. "Do you know where they went?"

"No. They left last night, and they're not coming back."

I swallow, staring at him without letting any emotion show on my face. It's like his words make so much sense and absolutely no sense at the same exact time. Why is telling me this? And why is he so calm about it? He's wrong.

Finally, finding my wits, I shake my head with a forced smile. "No. Clint wouldn't leave me. He's my boyfriend."

"You told me that last night." He's sitting in the chair

opposite me now, and I feel like a child under his stare, that disapproving expression painted on his face.

"I did?"

"Yes. While I walked you back to your room."

My spine straightens. He didn't bring me back. Clint did. I scan my memory, trying to remember whose arm I was on while I stumbled back, but I don't remember a face. Only an arm, and a sense of safety.

Oh, god.

It all comes crashing down on me like the ceiling just gave out. I've only known Clint for a few days. He's not my boyfriend. He's a complete stranger. And he has everything of mine. My money, my phone, my credit cards. My *passport.*

Oh, god. Oh, fuck. Oh, shit.

My eyes travel up to meet the man in the chair, and I can tell by the annoyed way his face twists in concern, he knows what I now know. I am royally fucked.

"But why?" I cry, placing my face in my hands.

"It's a common scam. Let me guess, you paid for the rental car."

"Oh my God!" I scream into my hands.

No, no, no. Clint cared about me. We had a connection. I let him come in me.

"I'll phone the police," the man says as he stands. "You can report the car stolen. You'll need to contact your banks and the US embassy to request a replacement passport."

His tone is almost scolding, and paired with the words coming out of his mouth, it's like ignition for my tears. Suddenly, I'm sobbing into my hands. This can't be happening. It's all a bad dream. This kind of stuff doesn't happen to me.

I keep waiting to wake up again, and the next time I do, I'll be curled cozily next to the man of my dreams instead of facing Mr. Tall, Cold, and Stoic. I peek through my tear-soaked fingers long enough to catch the look he's giving me before he stands up and walks to the desk. It's the kind of look an adult gives a naive child who didn't listen when they were told the stove was hot. It's the same look my much wiser, younger sister gives me everytime I end up broken-hearted after she warned me.

What the hell am I going to do now? I have nothing. No money, passport, car, or clothes. Is this how I end up homeless in Ireland? Are they going to kick me out because I can't pay them?

Anyone else in this situation might choose to toughen up, face the problem, and figure it out. But me, I choose to cry a little more and avoid looking at the asshole behind the counter.

The police woman has kind eyes, and she keeps touching my arm whenever I start to feel too frantic. She's been sitting with me in the hotel for over an hour, asking me everything about Clint and his friends. Of course, I don't know his last name or the names of his friends.

It almost irritates me how nice she is about it.

The woman who checked us in last night finally comes back and gets the story from the jerk in black. I watch from my chair across from the police woman as he tells her everything, and I find myself wondering if they're married, and I try to imagine how they ended up together. Did she feel the same way I felt about Clint? Starry-eyed and dreaming about a future owning a hotel together? Is he dependable and trustworthy so that she never has to wonder if he really loves her? Is he good in bed or is he a boring fuck who only likes missionary and never makes her climax?

I bet he's one of those hidden kink guys who likes to be called daddy and walks her around on a leash.

"Ma'am?" the police woman asks, grabbing my attention.

"Sorry, yeah?"

"You'll need to go to the US embassy. It's in Dublin. Here is the address. They can get you a replacement for your passport."

"I…" The words get stuck somewhere in my throat. I'm the most helpless human being in the world. I can't eat, sleep, or travel anywhere without someone's help.

"Yes, dear?" she asks, leaning forward with her round blue eyes and freckled cheeks.

"I'll take you," a voice bellows from behind me. I turn to find Mr. Green Eyes standing there with his hands in his pockets.

"Ah, thank you, Fa—"

"It's fine," he says quickly, cutting her off. I realize at this point that I don't even know his name, and he wants to take me on a road trip.

"You don't have to do that," I reply. I have literally no idea where Dublin is from here, but just the idea of traveling in a car down the road with that dark glare makes me want to cry.

"I know I don't, but how else are you going to get there?"

He's got me there. I am literally out of options.

"Thank you," I say, looking up at him and noticing the way he's focusing more on the police officer than me. I keep waiting for him to tell me his name, but he almost looks like he's avoiding me on purpose.

After the police woman leaves, I stand awkwardly in the lobby. I need to call my sister, but I no longer have a phone. Asking to call another continent isn't exactly an easy request, but even if they let me log onto their computer, I could DM her on Facebook or something.

Luckily, I don't have to stand around awkwardly for long. The woman leans across the counter and takes my hand. "You poor thing," she croons with her Irish lilt. "Do you want to call someone back home? Let them know you're okay?"

"Can I?"

"Of course!"

As she hands me the phone, I hold it in my hand, mentally preparing myself to call my sister. My sweet, self-less, has-her-life-together sister. Three years younger than me and she's already married with more potential in her future than I could ever dream of. This would never happen to Sunny.

The look on my face must be enough to clue the woman behind the counter in on the fact that I need privacy, so she walks away while I dial the number.

Within a few minutes, I hear Sunny's sleepy voice as she answers. I forgot about the time difference. It's only around noon here which means it's around 4:00 a.m. there.

"Hello," she croaks.

"Sunny." My voice comes out in a choked sob. Something about hearing my sister's voice breaks me. It's a reminder that she's so far away, and that I am practically on another planet.

"Cadence?" Her voice is full of concern, like she's suddenly wide awake.

"I'm so stupid," I say quietly, the tears finally cascading down my cheeks when I squeeze my eyes shut.

"What are you talking about? Where are you?"

"I'm somewhere in Ireland. I fucked up, Sunny."

"What do you mean 'somewhere in Ireland?'" she

responds. I hear a deep voice in the background quietly asking her questions. Her husband, Alexander, always had me pegged for the least reliable of the two of us.

Taking a deep breath, I try not to sound as shitty as I feel saying these words out loud. "I met someone."

There's silence on the line. That's all I need to say and Sunny knows that whoever this someone is, he's the reason I'm crying, lost in a foreign country. "Oh, Cadence."

"He took everything. My money, my passport, my rental car."

"Jesus," she mumbles. "Where are you now? Are you safe?"

I glance up at the cozy bed and breakfast. My eyes find the tall man who stands by the front door with the female police officer. He has ashy blonde hair and green eyes, weathered with a little age and a life of hard work. All things considered, I could be in much worse condition.

"Yeah, I'm safe," I answer. "I'm at a B&B on the beach. I guess things could be worse." A breathy laugh escapes my lips.

"Stay there," Sunny answers. "Send me their info. I'll send them money to cover your expenses while you figure out what you're going to do next."

My back starts to shake as another bout of sobs fight their way out. I've never felt like such an idiot in my whole life. My sister has to take care of me, why? Because I'm the world's biggest fuck up.

Something about her words registers. *While you figure out what you're going to do next.* Why wouldn't I just come home? What else would I do?

"Cadence, maybe this is a sign. Maybe you're alone right now because you need to be alone for a while."

My tears stop and my brow furrows. "I don't know how to be alone, Sunny."

16

"I know you don't, but you're stronger than you think, Cadence. You just spend too much time focusing on someone else when you should be focusing on yourself."

I have to bite my lip to fight off the tears again. She's right. Before Clint, it was Fischer. Before him, Liam. A procession line of fuckboys that went back as far as the English monarchy.

I am never alone. The thought makes my skin crawl. It doesn't just sound boring as fuck, but it's terrifying. What am I going to find if I look in the mirror? What will I find out about myself if I spend the next two weeks alone? What if I can't stand myself?

Just then I look up from the counter and see the nameless man staring at me again.

"Send me their information, okay?" Sunny adds before she yawns.

"I will. And I'll pay you back as soon as I can."

"Oh I'm not paying for it," she says with a raspy giggle, and I know she means that she'll be calling our dad when she's off the phone with me. Sunny and Alexander have more money than a thousand dads, but she's on a mission of retribution when it comes to the man who left us high and dry for a life with his secretary.

"Thanks, Sunny," I mumble, feeling the effects of the hangover coming back.

"You're welcome. Everything will be fine."

Before I hang up, she calls my name again. Putting the phone back up to my ear, I wait for her to speak.

After a heavy breath, she whispers into the phone. "Just focus on yourself. Stay away from the guys."

# Chapter 3

## Cadence

I spend the rest of the day in bed, sleeping off a physical and emotional hangover.

The next morning, I come downstairs to find a few of the other guests gathering around the parlor for breakfast.

"Oh, there you are," the red-head hotel owner says as she meets me in the lobby. "We tried to send dinner up to you last night, but I think you were sleeping."

My stomach growls at the sound. The truth is, I'm starving. I didn't eat a thing all day yesterday, and the smell of eggs and ham from the kitchen has my body screaming with hunger pangs.

The woman is quick to the kitchen to dish me up a plate of food, and I can barely force out a smile as I sit down and dig in.

"I got your sister's Venmo last night too."

My face lights up. Thank God for Sunny.

"It's enough for at least a two week's stay, plus extra for

food and clothes. Well, that's what she said. I can give you the extra in Euros after breakfast."

"Thank you," I mumble with my mouth full.

"I'm Bridget, by the way. My brother, Callum, has Mass today, but if you want to wait for him, he can take you into Shannon to get anything you can't get here. But maybe you'd like to explore Ennis a bit."

Her brother.

I don't know why that piece of information interests me, but I'm not exactly surprised he's at church while she's here. He seems exactly like the stick-up-the-ass church-goer I'd expected him to be.

This breakfast is probably the most delicious thing I've ever eaten, and along with a cup of sugared-up coffee, it's almost enough to knock off the cobwebs of yesterday's drama.

After my belly is full, Bridget takes me by the hand to the back of the house where her room is. She's being so nice to me, and I'm mortified. My best guess is she's about ten years older than me, but she's gorgeous with wild red hair and green eyes, exactly the kind of woman you'd expect to meet in Ireland.

She gives me a clean change of clothes; thankfully we wear the same size. Then, she pulls out the extra money Sunny transferred over in cash and hands it to me with a sad smile.

"It's a short walk to town. I'm afraid there's not a lot there, but there's a store there where you can at least get something of your own."

"Thank you," I mutter.

"Alright, take this road up about a kilometer and when you get to the end, turn right and head straight for the church. When you see the church, turn left. Then you'll be at the row of shops and grocers."

Looking down at the black leggings and tank top, I search for any semblance of myself. I'm not the kind of girl who throws pity parties for herself, and I throw lots of parties. But right now, even I'm having a hard time not feeling sorry for myself. I fall in love too easily...is that such a bad thing?

As I step out of the house, I'm faced with the breath-taking view of the beach again. Just out the front door of the B&B, there is a grassy yard met with a short drop to the long gray beach. For a moment, I can do nothing but stare at it. I bet Sunny would love this. She'd sketch it in one of her notebooks.

As for me, I just keep reaching for my phone that I no longer own, and it's making me shake with how much I miss it. On any other occasion, I'd snap a pic, upload it to Instagram with some vanity hashtag meant to appear humble and gracious.

With my sister's money folded up in the pocket of someone else's pants, I turn and follow Bridget's directions, walking along the coast. When the road ends, I make the right turn and see the church far ahead.

Probably wouldn't hurt for me to stop in there. That's if I don't burst into flames when I pass the doorway. I'm not a religious person. I don't even know if I believe in God, but I bet it's nice to have faith in something. Maybe if I had unwavering belief that God was by my side, I wouldn't feel so fucking alone all the time.

When I turn left at the church, I see the row of stores ahead, and like a beacon from God himself, the golden arches at the end of the street shine like the pearly gates of St. Peter. Ireland could have the most delicious food in the world, but right now I want to stuff my face with some-thing that tastes like home.

Yeah, I guess you could call it stress eating, and

honestly, I deserve that Big Mac and fries. And while I'm sitting down devouring it without an ounce of guilt, I let my conversation with Sunny replay through my head.

I need to focus on myself for a while, and she pretty strictly said that no guys should be involved. It's not like I'm listening to my twenty-one year old sister like she's my mother, but she's right. That's what I need. A break from men. A break from constantly trying to find love.

I guess that also means a break from sex, which is the thought coursing through my head as I devour all twelve hundred calories of this lunch. It's the closest thing I'm going to get to a good orgasm anytime soon.

It really is time to *focus on myself.*

I laugh quietly to myself and look up just in time to see a young group of guys looking my way. They're rugged looking, maybe fisherman, but with those strong jawlines and broad shoulders, I could get down with a little ruggedness.

One of the guys waves at me and sends me a smile that could charm a nun.

This is going to be harder than I thought. Quickly, I toss my garbage in the bin and hightail it out of the restaurant.

I find some basic jeans and cheap T-shirts at a little boutique off a side road. Taking my shopping bags, I start to realize just how much more I actually notice when I'm not buried in my phone while I walk. There are birds chirping and ocean waves. Straight ahead, I can hear the simple sounds of hymns coming from the church. The buildings are all different, some looking a hundred years older than the one right next to it, and they're all squeezed together like someone shoved them into one giant building.

Once I get to the church, where I'm supposed to turn right toward the main road, I stop on the corner and listen to the music for a moment. I can't understand a word of what they're singing, as it's accompanied by an organ, which overpowers the voices.

It's calming as fuck. And right now, I need calming, so instead of going back to the hotel where I have absolutely nothing to do, I take a seat on the low stone wall around the church.

Once the song stops, there is silence. A long silence. And finally a man says something, and the small crowd repeats something back to him. It sounds like a prayer.

A deep voice says something low and flat. At this point, I almost get up to leave. It sounds boring and I can't understand his muffled voice anyway, but then his words catch my attention.

"Sir, Son of David, take pity on me. My daughter is tormented by a devil."

My ears perk up. This just got interesting. As he continues on, it becomes clear that he's reading a story from the Bible, and I step closer to hear the rest. I'm just inside the front door but out of anyone's view. As I step into the church, the first thing I notice is the way it smells, like old wood and stone.

The second thing I notice is the way the priest's voice echoes through the space, bouncing off of every surface inch and pane of stained glass to land directly at my ears.

"But the woman had come up and was kneeling at his feet. 'Lord,' she said 'help me.' He replied, 'It is not fair to take the children's food and throw it to the house dogs.'"

*Damn, Jesus.* A smile stretches across my face as I listen to the story.

"She retorted, 'Ah yes, sir; but even house dogs can eat the scraps that fall from their master's table.' Then Jesus answered her, 'Woman, you have great faith. Let your wish be granted.' And from that moment her daughter was well again."

A low chuckle slips out through my lips just as the priest's voice cuts out. It's a tiny church, and I'm quite sure someone heard me judging by the long silence, so I press myself against the wall and out of sight.

Finally the priest starts talking again, going on and on about this passage and how it can be interpreted, and I wait for my opportunity to step out without being seen.

Then, his voice takes on a deeper tone, and the hair on my neck stands. I know that voice. Peeling myself away from the wall, I peer into the church, past the barely filled pews, and I stare in shock at the man speaking behind a podium.

He's in a heavy green robe draped over his broad shoulders that hangs down to his wrists. He's no longer wearing the cold expression he shared with me all day yesterday, but it's still the same man. Those ashy blond waves and full lips. I feel a fluttering in my belly as he stares at me from the end of the long aisle.

He doesn't take his eyes away for a long time, and I feel as if I'm the only person in the room. At the very least, I become the most important person in the room. The most interesting. The most special.

With a twitch in his eye that even I can spot from here, he flicks his hand toward the pews as if to tell me to sit, and had he not done that, I would have left. Instead, I walk quietly to the back row and rest against the hardwood. You'd really think after a thousand years of Christianity, they'd accommodate their believers a little better with softer seats.

But I'm too captivated by the man at the front with the charm and charisma in his speech from a man I've only known so far to show, at best, cold indifference. How the

Sara Cate

hell is this the same man who sat at the bar two nights ago? Who delivered me my shitty news yesterday?

I didn't know a priest could have a life outside the church. Drink at a pub. What the hell do I know? I haven't set foot in a church since my aunt's wedding when I was thirteen, and I was too busy ogling my hot soon-to-be-step-cousin to pay any attention to anything spiritual going on.

"Let us think about the woman in this verse. The foreigner. Tortured by a devil. Desperate for salvation, begging for help from our Savior."

My cheeks burn as his gaze keeps landing back on my face, but I am tied to his words like the string of a kite. As he continues about the woman in the scripture, I feel like I can't move.

Everytime he lifts an arm, that heavy robe draped from his arm like a sail, I inhale for a desperate breath. And I feel every word, every lilt and sound in his words run down my spine like fire. I could listen to him speak up there for hours.

My thighs clench when his gaze lands on me again, and I wonder what those robes would feel like between my fingers. Between my legs.

I find myself picturing him without the robes, how it would feel to peel them away, revealing the man beneath. It makes me wonder if a man in his position could resist the allure of a woman, the promise of sex.

Jesus. I need to get out of here.

It's about that time that everyone starts standing up and walking toward the front. They kneel in front of him, and he says something to each of them that I can't understand, but I quickly sneak out the door I came in. I don't know if he saw me leave or not.

It felt like I was imposing on something intimate and

24

private. And now he's going to think I'm a Catholic and invite me to their Sunday service or whatever it's called.

But I'd be lying if I didn't admit that my shoulders do feel a little lighter after being in there. Fuck, who knows. Maybe I need a little Jesus in me, and I'll stop being such a fuck up.

Once outside, I set my bags down to readjust them on my arms. There's a community bulletin board by the stairs leading down to the street, and I swear I don't believe in fate and signs, but after today, I just might.

Just as I look up, I see a piece of paper:

*Help Wanted at Ennis Beach Bed & Breakfast. Front desk and maintenance skills required.*

It's one of those crazy ideas that doesn't really have an argument against it other than it's crazy.

No.

That's my initial reaction. I pick up my bags and head back down the main street toward the hotel. I'm getting my replacement passport this week. I'll get a flight home next week and life will be back to normal.

I'll move back in with Mom. Maybe get a new job in Pineridge. Something fun and easy like a server at the sports bar. I don't need the money, but it would get me out of the house. Maybe there's a hotel in Pineridge that would hire me.

I can't work here at this hotel.

I can't.

That's fucking insane.

And yet, when I walk into the house, Bridget smiles at me from behind the counter.

"Got yourself a little something, then?"

I don't answer her. Instead, I blurt out, "You're hiring?"

The words just fall out of my mouth, and I don't even

mean them to, but I guess my mouth knows what my brain can't accept. I don't want to go back to Pineridge. I don't want to go back to my life.

There is absolutely no reason I can't work here at this hotel.

"Ummm…" Bridget is shocked to silence. "Yes, we are."

"What about a room available? Somewhere I could stay longer than a week?"

I'm shocked her eyebrows can even go higher than they already are, but somehow she pulls it off. "Actually...there is."

My heart is beating so fast, I have to swallow down this ball of nerves building in my throat. I've lost my goddamn mind. I haven't even put my fucking bags down.

"Can I apply?" I say, squaring my shoulders.

"You want to work here?"

"Yes."

"Well, don't you want to know about the position?" she asks, looking almost hopeful.

"I guess. Yeah." My mouth is moving at a speed twenty times faster than my brain.

"We need someone to help clean the rooms, tidy up after breakfast, and help Callum out in the barn."

"The barn?" My heart drops at that mention. I can clean a hotel room. This place is tidy anyway. But working in a barn? I can't do that…

Sunny's words echo back like a defense. *You are stronger than you think.*

Fuck.

"I can do that," I answer with far less confidence than she probably wants to see.

"Wonderful," she says, clapping her hands together. I

don't know if she's excited that she's getting interest in the job or because it's me, but her excitement is contagious.

Too bad her next words make me want to take it all back.

"You'll have to do an interview with Callum since he does the hiring."

I want to tell her that I'm supposed to be staying away from men, especially charmers who are too hot to be priests and have already seen me blackout drunk. I can't sit through an interview with him, not after I just snuck out of his speech at the church where I basically imagined what he looked like naked through the whole thing.

I'm supposed to be focusing on me, but how can I do that when he's everywhere I turn?

# Chapter 4

## Callum

"You've got to be fucking kidding me." Staring down at my phone, I wince as soon as the words come out. My voice doesn't travel far, but I take a cautious glance around the corner, watching the back door for any movement as I quickly stub out my cigarette and toss it into the can I keep back here, hiding my bad habit behind the flowerpot.

I really need to learn to watch my mouth while I'm here, but this text from my sister threw me for a loop. Plus, I'm still nursing a forty-eight hour headache from hell. I don't usually go to Yeager's on weekend nights, but I wanted to keep an eye on that group that checked into the house. My instincts are usually right about this stuff, and sometimes I hate to be right.

I sure as shit didn't see this coming.

The girl wants to work at the house.

The girl I carried to her room two nights ago after I found her passed out in the corner booth of the pub. With those heart-shaped lips and tits like temptation, I had a feeling this one would be trouble.

I feel bad for her, I really do, but she fell for that scam like a child, and that's not someone I need hanging around all the time. I know Bridget is getting attached already. She's lonely, I get it, but half the shit I need this girl to do involves cleaning out Misty's stable and keeping up the grounds.

I'd venture to guess this girl hasn't mowed a lawn in her life.

My phone won't stop pinging with Bridget's texts.

*This could be good for business.*
   *Guests would love her.*
   *I need another woman around here.*
   *Someone fun!*
   *Unlike you.*

Yeah, yeah, yeah.

It wasn't supposed to be this way. My sister and her husband took over the bed and breakfast from our grandparents. It was their dream. But right in the middle of my seminary, my brother-in-law had a pint too many, got behind the wheel, and never made it home.

Now it feels like I'm the one being torn in two.

The urge to tell her no is overpowering, but what's more overpowering is the desire to let her be happy for a fucking second. After everything, she deserves this. A shitty employee if it makes her smile.

*We'll talk about it at dinner.*

.   .   .

That's really the nicest I can be, and she accepts it with an enthusiastic THANK YOU.

When I get to the house that night, the girl's voice is the first thing I hear. It's nothing like the despondent victim I saw yesterday. Now she's chattering on with Bridget in the kitchen about some restaurant in California where they cook on the table.

I stop in the foyer, pausing to hear her rattle on.

There's a joyful lilt in her tone as she laughs at her own jokes, Bridget falling in line and giggling as they both carry dishes out to the table. This is the person who will help me with the stables and fixing the toilets. This is a fucking joke.

My niece, Daisy, is already at the table, staring down at her phone. Every few seconds she glances up and lets a subtle smile slip into her usually melancholy features. When she sees me, I lift my eyebrows at her, as if I caught her in the act of looking anything but downright despondent.

My sister and Cadence don't spot me right away, so I clear my throat, stopping Cadence right in the middle of her story.

"Oh," she says with her round blue eyes focused right on me.

"Callum." My sister says my name as if it's required to acknowledge my presence. My eyes don't leave the girl. Her long dark hair is pulled up in a messy bun on top of her head, exposing the nape of her neck, and I count the three vertebraes on her back before the rest disappear in her loose T-shirt.

Quickly, I busy myself with the papers on the counter, checking for bills and messages. The girls go back to the kitchen, and I hear Cadence carry on with her conversation. My sister's laugh echoes through the house like the walls are hungry for it. It blows away the dust that has settled since Teddy died.

I'd be a real asshole to deny her this. To tell her she can't hire this complete stranger who landed on our doorstep twenty-four hours ago.

Am I a terrible brother for saying no to this request? Or am I a pitiful man if I put my family in danger? For all we know, this girl is a scammer, here to rob us blind.

I know she's not. I saw it in the sincerity of her tears yesterday morning. The fear and the panic was real, but it's up to me to be cautious.

"Come eat, Callum." Bridget sets the dishes on the table and finds her place next to Cadence who sits at the corner across from Daisy. I take the seat at the head with her on my right. Her bare knee bumps mine as I sit down.

She begins scooping up my sister's shepherd's pie just as I clasp my hands and bow my head.

There are no hotel guests tonight. When there are, we invite them to eat with us. Not many do, but when they do, I keep the grace short and sweet. It makes some of our guests uncomfortable, which is why I see Bridget's head snap toward me when I start up with a zealous call to Our Heavenly Father.

"Oh, shit." The heavy spoon clangs against the dish interrupting my prayer as Cadence drops it to clasp her hands together. I glare at her from the corner of my eye. She awkwardly bows her head and mumbles an amen when I'm done. She might be a hotel guest, but she wants to work and live here, so she might as well get used to it.

Dinners are usually quiet. If we're not talking about business, the three of us will eat while scrolling through our phones, but Cadence breaks the silence every moment or so to talk about anything and everything. Her home in

California. Moments from her trip through Europe so far. Her up-and-coming artist sister.

I struggle to keep my eyes off her lips while she talks. There's something about the animated way they move, exposing her perfectly straight white teeth and the subtle dimple in her chin that is so disarming I forget that I'm not supposed to stare, and I'm especially not supposed to stare at beautiful women half my age.

The phone rings in the middle of one of her stories, and my sister jumps up to answer it, leaving me alone with my distant niece and this new stranger.

After a moment's silence, I turn toward her. "It was a surprise to see you in Mass today."

She doesn't respond, but in her defense, I didn't really say it was nice to see her, just a surprise.

"Are you Catholic?"

I spot a hint of a scoff while she takes a bite of her dinner and shakes her head. "Oh, no. I just heard the music, and I thought I'd check it out."

In my experience, people don't just "check out" Sunday Mass. She's being awkward with me, much more uptight than with my sister, but I can assume that up until today she didn't even know I was a priest. I understand it can throw people sometimes. The difference in the way they treat you is obvious. It's like I'm suddenly someone to avoid eye contact with and serve an overabundance of respect.

"And what did you think?"

Cadence's eyes widen and a thick awkwardness stains the air between us.

"Um...it was nice," she mutters without looking up at me.

She's clearly uncomfortable, but I don't know why I

want to know more. I want to hear what she thought of today's verse, the words I wrote, the wisdom I delivered.

This time, her eyes flick upward, meeting mine. Those round blue orbs seem so innocent and yet so intoxicating, like she's an angel, but the kind of angel who wants to fall from grace.

When Bridget returns to the table, everything starts to feel a lot less awkward. That is until she starts in on the topic I want to avoid so badly.

"So, when would you like to interview our one and only applicant for the job?"

My lips tense as I glance up at Cadence, who is now perky with interest. There's an actual fucking sparkle in her eye.

"Right now, I guess."

"I was kidding, Callum. Do you really need to interview her at all? It's such a lousy pay."

"What do you know about tending to horses? Cleaning stalls? General household maintenance?" My questions are aimed at Cadence, and I almost expect her to shrink back. I'm being harsh, too harsh, and I don't feel good about it, but I can't help my heels from digging themselves into this whole situation.

"I can learn. It can't really be that hard," Cadence answers coyly.

"You want to rake horse shit out of a stall for seventy-five euros a day?"

"Yes, I do." She's being proud and stubborn. It makes me want to be proud and stubborn too.

"You're not working here behind the counter with Bridget. I need someone in the barn, long hard hours. Mowing the lawn, tending to the landscaping. Driving the tractor and the mower."

33

"I can handle it," she answers with her shoulders squared. After a moment, a smile spreads across her cheeks leaving deep dimples on either side of those heart-shaped lips.

With a tone of resignation, I lean back and shake my head. "It's a man's job."

Her smile fades and she glares at me with the fire of the sun, her pouty lips hanging open.

"A man's job?" she shrieks. "What? Do you steer the lawn mower with your dick?"

Daisy chokes on her own laugh as Bridget slaps a hand over her mouth. My face doesn't change. I hold my cold, empty expression as she glares right back.

"Watch your mouth."

"Don't be a sexist," she quips back. "Plus you said shit."

It's because she said the words *your dick* to me, specifically those words: *your* and *dick*. Saying fuck and shit is one thing, but talking to a priest about his dick...at the dinner table no less, is what practically set the room a blaze. And I realize it was a metaphorical *your dick*, but my brain can't get past that exact phrase to make sense of it.

This interview isn't going well for either of us.

"I assume you two have discussed boarding."

"We have an extra room," my sister says in defense.

"Take it out of my pay." Cadence hasn't so much as blushed since the *your dick* moment. Can she see how unravelled I am?

"Listen," she says, leaning toward me with her hands folded on the table. "I don't care about the pay. I don't need it. I would just rather do anything in the world than go home to my boring life without a future. Anything."

Those crystal ocean blues are boring into me with a slight lift to one brow and a playful half-smile on her round lips. The other girls start giggling, and I know I've lost.

"Thirty days," I answer through clenched teeth. "You have thirty days. If you even make it that long."

"I guess I'll be applying for a work visa at the consulate on top of my passport." She stands from the table with a smile.

"I'll go make up your room," Bridget says with a wide grin as she starts picking up our plates. And as I struggle to look away from this firecracker of a girl sitting next to me, I'm afraid of what I just got myself into. Very afraid.

# Chapter 5

## Cadence

There's an empty room on the third floor that they don't use for guests. The first floor on the far back of the house is where Bridget and Daisy sleep. The second floor is strictly for guests with a small sitting room and a circle of doors around the staircase in the middle. On the top floor, there is a spare room for Callum when he chooses to sleep in it over the rectory at the church.

Then there is my spare room. It's an overflow room, Bridget says, but since their business has been down, they haven't put anyone in it in over a year. Still the staff keeps it clean. It's just next to the third floor bathroom which is small with a shower full of men's body wash and shampoo. No Irish Spring, to my disappointment.

Now it's my turn to wear the smug smile as I ascend the stairs with Bridget. She wasn't going to make me move upstairs yet, since I'm still technically a guest, but I insisted. I'm ready to move on. I don't want to wait.

It's not like I have anything to move with me anyway.

"Don't worry about my brother," Bridget says with a smile as she flips on the light to the small room with a slanted ceiling. There's a large window above the bed that looks out over the green field behind the hotel. The other side, Callum's room, must look out over the ocean. One house...two totally different views.

In the distance, I can make out a dirt road and a white barn. "I'm not worried about him," I answer. And I'm not. Callum is one of those men who feels the need to assert his authority for no other reason than he thinks he has to. He puffs his chest and hides behind this layer of masculinity that ensures no one truly sees his real emotions.

I know his type all too well. He's basically my father. Callum has his collar. My father has his money. It makes them essential, guarantees that someone will need them... because underneath they are afraid no one really wants them.

I despise my father. Always have. It was like I was born with a special pair of glasses that let me see through all the years of bullshit and lies. My little sister was a fool for his tricks. She depended on him so much that when he left, it broke her.

I celebrated.

"Callum just feels like he has to protect everyone all the time." Bridget is taking a dusting cloth around the room, even though it looks nearly perfect to me. I mean, I totally plan on spicing it up with something, but for now, it works.

"Well, he needs to lighten up if he's going to have me around."

She stops what she's doing and looks up at me. "Don't hold your breath. Callum takes everything too seriously. You know," she says, leaning against the white dresser. "If he wasn't a priest, I think he'd be into you."

A laugh bursts out of my chest. "Ha. He is not my type."

Bridget sits on the chair and I plop down on the bed. This intimacy of girl talk makes me miss my sister. "What is your type then?" she asks.

"Oh, gosh," I say with a dramatic flair. "Let's see...narcissistic, self-absorbed, manipulative, noncommittal....and hot. Always hot."

Bridget chuckles. "Aww...well, I know a few men around Ennis that you will love."

"No thanks. I promised my sister I'm focusing on me. No men."

She nods. "Good plan."


It doesn't take me long to fall asleep that night. The residual hangover allows for me to fall easily into a deep slumber, that is until I hear footsteps on the stairs. There's nothing in here to tell the time, no phone or alarm clock, but I'd have to guess that it's at least one or two in the morning.

The floor creaks with every step, and I quickly get up from my bed to take a peek out the door. The gentle squeak from the hinge makes the dark figure reaching the landing stop and turn back toward me.

Bridget said they don't use this floor for guests, so there's only one person who should be swaying in the darkness in the middle of the night. Our eyes meet, lit only by the moonlight shining through the sky light. He doesn't say anything, but I see something sad in his eyes.

He's drunk, and I almost feel sorry for him.

There's a distant thought as we stare at each other that reminds me that this could be a dangerous scenario if he were anyone else. If he wasn't a priest and maybe if he didn't despise me so much, I'd open my door for him. What I said to Bridget was true: he's not my type. He's rude and cold and hasn't shown the slightest interest in me.

Suddenly, he's taking long swaying steps toward me instead of toward his door on the opposite side. My heart thuds loudly in my chest as he steps so close to me that I can smell his whiskey-soaked breath on my face. Other than that, he smells good. So good, my mouth waters. Like smoke, cologne, and ocean air all mixed together.

I try to hide the heavy way my chest rises and falls with each breath, and just as I'm about to ask him what he's doing, he leans forward and presses one finger to his lips, signalling me to stay quiet.

*What is happening?* My mind screams.

With his bloodshot eyes leveled on my face, he brushes his thumb sloppily over my bottom lip. I pick up the bitter scent of cigarette smoke on his hands. I should move away. I definitely should *not* be letting him touch me or corner me in the dark, but I'm a deer in headlights. It's surreal, too weird. I can't look away. At the same time, I want him to see that he doesn't intimidate me.

Then, he leans forward, and I expect him to kiss me. If he does, will I let him? Will I kiss him back? Pull him into my room and let him between my legs?

For curiosity's sake, probably.

But he doesn't kiss me. Instead his mouth stops within an inch of my ear. His voice cuts through the silence, harsh and cruel, so loud in my ear I jolt. But it's not just the abrupt volume that hurts.

"Slut."

My breath stops. Heat floods my cheeks as I flinch, finally pulling away to glare at him. With a dead look in his stupid green eyes, he turns away and stumbles to his room, slamming against the wall on his way.

Sara Cate

That word hangs in the air while I stand in the doorway, looking around for anyone else who might have witnessed that. It's almost too insane to believe. The guy barely says anything to me, and then he chooses to hit me with this? I mean, I get that he's drunk, but I'm pretty sure he meant what he said.

On instinct, I want to tell Sunny. She's probably the one who would believe me that my boss, the mean priest, just called me a slut for absolutely no reason in the middle of the night while he was piss drunk.

Instead, I shut myself in my room, climb into bed, and try to shake off the pain of that single word. This isn't even close to being the first time someone spewed that word at me, but it's the first time it hurt. Maybe by his standards, I am a slut. Maybe he wants me to feel the shame of being who I am.

And it's not about the sex. I'm not going to apologize for loving sex, but fresh off the pain of being duped by Clint, I feel what he's trying to tell me. I'm just a stupid girl who opened her legs for a stranger and got what she deserved.

I want to scream into my pillow. I want to march over to his room and tell him that he doesn't have the right to talk to me that way, but I doubt it would make a difference. He's a stone wall, void of emotion. Besides, I'm not here for his pity. Like Sunny said, I'm tougher than I think, and there's no fucking way I'm going to let that asshole get to me.

## Chapter 6

### Cadence

"It's here!" Holding the thin piece of plastic in my hand feels like having a piece of my freedom I didn't know I'd been missing. The replacement credit card is just the first in many things that I need to replace since Clint the Cunt, as Bridget and I have named him, took everything I owned.

It's been seven days in the house, and already I feel at home. I've barely seen Callum at all since the *midnight slut-shaming* incident. He's been eating and sleeping at the rectory since. There have been guests checking in and out everyday, so I've been spending my days helping Bridget and Daisy with things around the house. I like having new people in the house for breakfast, and I especially love the idea of this being the only thing I have to do around here. Maybe if he doesn't come back, I won't have to worry about those other things he said the job entailed.

I've never stayed in a bed and breakfast before, so it's weird to me that a hotel would include sitting around a table together with complete strangers, but it seems to be so normal here. They can sit in the parlor at the various other tables if they choose, but I think they come for the experience. As Bridget has told me, the house has been in their family for generations and comes with more stories and history than I'll ever know.

"What's here?" asks a deep voice from behind me. Spinning around, I rest my back against the lobby counter and stare into the emerald eyes of Father Fuckface, in his full black outfit with the white collar. Even the middle of summer is pretty temperate here, but still, he must be hot in all that black. He keeps his sleeves rolled up to the elbows, but I still wonder how it must feel under those thick black pants.

"It's my credit card," I answer proudly.

"Going shopping?" There's a quizzical turn to his brow as he stares down at me. He's so much taller than me it's almost intimidating. I normally like super tall guys, but they usually aren't trying to be so dominating.

I've considered since that night that maybe he doesn't remember what he said to me or how close he got to me, but even Bridget said it wasn't like him to spend so long away from the house, so I assumed he remembered and was embarrassed.

Which makes me wonder why he thinks it's okay to talk to me like nothing happened now. I'm waiting for an apology that doesn't look like it's coming. Isn't that a Catholic thing? Asking for forgiveness.

Of course, I'd just tell him he could take his forgiveness and shove it straight up his ass.

"Maybe," I finally answer, looking anywhere but in those cold eyes.

"Not today. We have work to do."

Inwardly, I groan. I've been getting along so nicely

helping out inside the house with Bridget, but I knew I was dreaming. He'd be here to steal me away from all the joy and comfort any minute.

"Bridget can let you borrow her work boots for now," he says with a deep grumble.

He brushes past me to head for the kitchen. "I'm going to show you how to clean Misty's stable and feed her, which you'll need to do daily. Once a week, she needs brushing, and once you're comfortable with her, you'll have to give her some exercise."

It takes me a moment before I realize he's talking about a horse, and I feel my insides sour at the thought. It's not the first time he's mentioned a horse, but I was just sort of hoping we could avoid bringing it up again. I never even had a pet growing up, let alone a full-size horse. What's the point, anyway?

"Get dressed and meet me out in the van in fifteen minutes," he says.

"Are you working in that?" I gesture to his priest uniform, or whatever it's called. I don't know why I asked this or why I'm even entertaining the idea of a conversation with him, but the question slips out.

Glancing down, he shakes his head, then turns to stomp up the stairs. "Of course not." He scoffs like I'm an idiot. "We had a charity breakfast this morning."

A charity breakfast. Of course. He probably feeds the homeless and spoons oatmeal into the mouths of little old ladies to complete his bullshit holier-than-thou image.

He's in the van with the engine running when I emerge from the house with an old pair of boots and clothes from Bridget that are all a little too big. I need to buy work clothes, but I haven't the slightest idea where I would even do that.

As I climb in, I immediately notice the scent of his cologne, the memory of that night in the dark hitting me like a truck. Did he just put that on or does he always smell this good? I don't ask, but I turn my head away and inhale it, savoring the smell. I'm obsessed with men's cologne. Something about it just turns my gears, and I love how one scent can take you back. I can remember almost every man I've been with based on just their cologne.

But Callum's is different. It's fresh with something ancient-smelling and earthly. Hell, maybe it's frankincense from the church, but I kind of love it. Even if I can't stand him.

"I'll show you around the farm today, and you can get started with Misty."

We take a gravel path that you couldn't even call a road toward the barn in the middle of the field. I spot the black and white horse about halfway down the road. I watch Callum out of the corner of my eye as he leans against the open window and keeps that subtle scowl in his brow. It's like he's always thinking of ways he hates me.

As we pull up to the barn, he throws the truck into park and hops out, shouting toward the horse who comes trotting up toward him. Something keeps me stuck in place as I watch the animal approach him, rubbing its nose against his chest.

When he turns to look for me, I cower farther down into the van. "Aren't you going to put it in the stable?" I ask.

Callum ignores me and turns to the horse, gently stroking her nose and mumbling something to her in a way that is almost gentle. Carefully, I open the door and stand still as stone by the truck.

"She's gentle. Come here." He holds a hand out toward me with one on the horse's nose.

The intensity in his expression and the way his accent creates a little flutter in my gut has me inching my feet toward him. For some reason, I actually take his calloused hand as he guides me toward the horse. She's probably not the biggest horse, but she still towers over me. With a nudge to my arm, she breathes out, a gust of air through her nostrils hitting my chest.

A high-pitched squeak comes out, and Callum's grip on my hand tightens. "Relax."

He positions himself behind me, putting me between the horse and him. My heart is beating rapidly in my chest as he guides my hand down the animal's nose then her mane. She barely reacts as I run my fingers through her long black hair.

Slowly, I begin to relax. The warmth of Callum's hands over mine is a complete dichotomy from the man who insulted me a few days ago. He has so much confidence with the animal, but exhibits a gentle but firm side that keeps Misty calm. Fuck, it's keeping me calm too.

That is until I feel Callum abandon me and I see him walking over to the barn, leaving me alone with the horse.

"What the fuck are you doing?" I gasp, forgetting my filter.

He doesn't answer, just turns back with a pail full of what looks like soft apples. Disappointment written all over his features—probably from my language—he drops an apple in my hand.

He returns to his place at my back and he leans against me, pushing my hand to the horse's mouth.

Goosebumps break out across my back as I take in his scent, close enough to overpower the horse's less than appealing odor. Without letting him see, I swallow and bite my lip to keep from letting it hang open.

His body is flush against mine, and I'm sure this has to be against the priest rules. I guess as long as he isn't enjoying it, it's okay to help a young woman feed an apple to a horse.

Even if he thinks she's a slut.

Each time Misty takes an apple from my hands, I ease into a new level of comfort. Like he can sense it, Callum steps away. I risk a glance in his direction, searching for any sign that being so close to me had any effect on him, nerves or discomfort or stiff jeans, but he moves around the barn, picking up rakes and shovels looking a little too nonchalant for my liking. If I stood that close to any other guy, I'd at least notice something in him change.

"Every morning, you need to come out here and make sure Misty has water and fresh hay. Every other day, her stall needs mucking. The floor needs sweeping, and she'll need exercise around the yard."

"Okay." I keep feeding apples to Misty like a robot. I'm afraid if I stop, she'll start eating me instead.

"Come here, Cadence."

As he turns and disappears into the barn, I let the sound of my name on his lips course through my mind again and again. The gentle way it rolls off his tongue makes me hate him a little more. I'd prefer he go back to calling me slut so that at least I can compartmentalize my feelings for him more clearly.

Carefully, I step away from the horse and drop the bucket on the same box I saw him retrieve it from.

He shows me the different steps to caring for Misty and cleaning her stable, tending to the small garden behind the barn and keeping up with the grass. It's not much, and none of it seems beyond my abilities, but I know this is only half of it. I still have work to do at the house too. I wonder how long I'll be working each day and how all of this labor is going to feel after a few days. I don't work out much, and I certainly don't do a lot of work like this.

After we leave Misty, he takes me back to the house. There's a small shed behind the house, and he takes me through the lawn maintenance I'm supposed to do there.

By this time, it's past noon, and my stomach is grumbling. I'm having a hard time focusing on what he's saying, but he just keeps droning on and on with instructions, and I know that I'm not retaining any of it. I'll get the hang of it when I actually do it. I can't remember it all now.

"Are you listening to me?"

I look up from the ocean view to see his face, red-cheeked and sweat beading on his brow from the sun.

"Aren't you hungry?" I ask.

"We'll eat after we go through this."

He catches me rolling my eyes at him, and I watch his jaw clench. Suddenly, I know for a fact that he remembers the night in the dark. It's in the disappointed expression on his face. I feel like a child about to be scolded.

"Please remember you're here to work, not to mess around. This isn't a game. This is our business, our home. If you won't take it seriously, then I'll be the first to put you back on a plane to California. Before your thirty days is done if I have to."

The air has grown stiff and awkward between us while I grovel, biting my lip and hating him like I used to hate my dad for talking down to me.

And the same thoughts repeat in my mind, like a silent anthem to myself.

*You're wrong about me. You're wrong about me. You're wrong about me.*

He thinks I'm a spoiled princess, a slut, a stupid girl

47

who can't do anything. A rich California millennial afraid to get her hands dirty. I refuse to be belittled and treated like an idiot. I won't tell him what a jerk he's being or how wrong he is.

I'll show him.

# Chapter 7

## Cadence

There are tendrils of sweat dripping down my back as I climb the stairs that evening, desperate for a shower. After lunch, Callum and I raked out the dead garden beds behind the house. I didn't even know Ireland could be hot until today.

After we finished the first one together, him correcting my every move, he left me to finish the second by myself. Still I felt like he was watching me the entire time I raked and shoveled and pulled the weeds out of that bed. I could hear him in my head, telling me how I was doing it wrong, how lazy I was, how wrong I was for this job. I cursed his name in my mind the entire time I worked and imagined every weed I pulled from the ground was his head.

Still, I found myself wishing he would come back out and work alongside me.

But he never came back outside after he left me with the work, so I packed up the garden supplies when I was done and dumped the wheelbarrow in the compost all by myself like he told me to. He probably has work to do at the church, which would explain his absence.

I didn't even know priests could have other jobs, but I guess this isn't really a job as much as responsibility. He's here to help out his sister since she lost her husband. It's not like he's an entrepreneur looking to get rich.

I do wish they'd let me give them more tips on the hotel. This has to be one of the most beautiful locations in the world and they haven't been fully booked in over a year. It doesn't make sense.

If they would just update the place a little, list it on some more current apps, they would be booming with business. And Ennis isn't a bad town for young travelers. The beach isn't like a regular beach with waves and sun, but that's what makes it better. It's all about the novelty of something authentic and different. If they could market that, they would make a killing. But I've only been here a couple days and I don't want to insert myself too soon.

As I reach the top of the stairs, I decide to just get straight into the shower instead of dragging all of this dead grass and dirt to my room. I can smell myself, and I don't want this stench anywhere near where I sleep. So once I reach the top of the stairs, I take the two steps to the bathroom and throw open the door.

My heart stops in my chest.

Standing in the middle of the room, bent over the sink with shaving cream on his face is Callum—and the shaving cream is the *only* thing on his body. The *only thing.* My eyes can't help themselves as they travel down from his shocked expression across those thick biceps and ridged abs to the thing hanging between his legs. I should not be looking, and really it's only a split second, but it's etched into my memory, and I'm still staring at it. I'm not just staring, I'm drinking it in, gawking, sketching it on paper like my sister does when she tells me to freeze. It's half hidden by a gentle tuft of black hair, but even as he turns away I catch the way it hangs with a little bit of life and not completely dead and flaccid. In my not so limited experience with men, I've learned that this means my new boss has relieved himself recently.

"Jesus Christ!" he bellows as he snatches a towel and covers himself in a rush.

I shouldn't smile, but he turns so quickly, hiding himself from my view so that my vision is left with his porcelain white bum just as I slam the door shut.

I can't move. Standing outside the bathroom, I just keep this polaroid picture of naked Callum in my brain, like it's slowly developing and mine to keep forever.

Slapping my hand over my mouth, I turn and scurry to my room, trying to stifle my laugh as I slam my door shut with me behind it.

Jumping onto my bed, forgetting that I'm filthy and covered in dirt, I quickly shut my eyes, soaking in that vision although I'm not sure if I want it or not.

I'm not attracted to Callum—not like that. He's a priest. Too old for me, and not rich enough to make being old cool. Too much of an asshole half the time. I barely know him…sure I've known guys far less and seen a great deal more, but still. Why am I still thinking about him naked?!

Suddenly, he's in my doorway, and I can't bear to open my eyes.

"If we're going to share a bathroom, you should really learn to knock."

Still, my eyes are clenched shut. "Don't you live at the church?"

"Sometimes. But as far as you're concerned, you can assume I live across the hall and will occasionally be naked

51

in the bathroom with the door closed. I'll assume the same about you."

"I'm sorry," I mumble, now covering my entire face with my hands. I can't look at him. I can't. Not with these new feelings stirring around in my head, like the vision of him naked was some kind of fuel to the fire.

After a pause, I peek my eyes open to see if he's still there, and I wish I hadn't. Because he is still there, in a pair of jeans...without a shirt. Still glistening from the shower and looking a little too ripped for a clergyman.

He looks like he wants to say something.

"Twenty-five Hail Mary's for seeing your priest naked."

I stare at him, mouth hanging open. "Wh—what?"

"Thirty if you entertained lustful thoughts."

"Oh my God!"

My shriek bounces off the old wood and stained windows as I slam my face back in my hands. He says it with the most serious expression, and I can't tell if he's kidding or if I'm hallucinating.

Finally, he does leave, and I can open my eyes. But I cannot forget the way he looked, standing in my doorway trying to punish me for seeing him naked. I don't know what the fuck a Hail Mary is, but I have a feeling I'll need to do a lot more than thirty with the way I'm thinking right now.

# Chapter 8

## Callum

It doesn't normally take me this long to write a homily, but I've been distracted all week. Tonight we have Mass, and this thing is half-written. Before I toss my laptop out the window, I sneak out the back entrance for a much needed vice break. When the smoke hits my lungs, my shoulders relax.

I used to do my writing at the house, but now she is there all the time, and I can't seem to get anything down on paper when she's around.

We get a lot of girls like Cadence at the B&B. Young, enthusiastic, strong-willed. They don't stick around for long, and they don't normally have this effect on me.

I've never second-guessed my decision to take my vows. I wanted to devote myself to something bigger than me, something that would be around after I was gone, and I never considered myself a romantic guy anyway. I dated and even fell in love in my twenties—when I was her age, and it always left me feeling empty and unfulfilled.

This...speaking to my congregation, living in divinity and sacrament, feeling the presence of God in everything I do...this fulfills me.

Do these things by any means make me a good person...I wish. That's what I thought when I took my vows. I was doing right. I was *being* righteous. Moral compass be damned, I needed straight and narrow rules, and the holy orders give me that.

Sure, I have my vices, but I'm upstanding where it counts.

But fuck. Passing by that girl every morning and every night, watching her hoist a shovel in those short shorts, sweat glistening on her sun-kissed skin, knowing she's sleeping so close to me and just within my reach, it's doing things to me.

Maybe that's why I called her a slut when I was drunk. Not that that's by any means an excuse. I know how fucked up that was, but maybe if she had better self-restraint in the first place, she wouldn't have landed in my B&B without a penny to her name.

Living under my roof. Sleeping next door.

I would never break my vow. I wouldn't. I'm not that kind of man, but it doesn't stop me from thinking about it. No matter how sinful those thoughts are.

It's a temptation. I know that. Just a test of my faith and commitment, and thinking about sinning is the same as sinning. A better priest wouldn't do even that, but I'm not a great priest. I'm not a terrible one, and I follow the rules for the most part. My sermons bring in more followers. We've turned the church around in the community, and our volunteer contributions have quadrupled since I took the position.

How bad is it if I spend my nights thinking about the way Cadence might sound when she comes? Or what her favorite position is. Or what those full lips would feel like around my cock.

I'll say another Hail Mary for that last one. That was too much.

It's like she's found her way inside my mind without my permission.

As I head back inside, I make a quick stop in the bathroom to wash my hands and spray on a little cologne to cover the smoke. The ladies who usually help set up for Mass will be here in an hour, and I don't want to smell like an ashtray.

Sitting back down to my desk, I exhale.

Focus. Write this homily.

Or recycle one from a few years ago…

Just as I open my laptop to dig into some of my old stuff, I hear a knock on my office door.

"It's open," I call.

As she pushes open the door, I see her out of my periphery and I know those long legs before I can even glance up. She insists on wearing shorts with the long work boots coming up to her mid-shins. The bottoms of her pockets peek out of her cut-offs, and I feel the need to mentally apologize to the statue of Mary, poised behind me like she can see the thoughts in my head.

I would only have to shift the inseam of those shorts a little to the side…

Stop it.

Cadence steps in and looks around my office, and I see that she's a little tense, maybe a tad uncomfortable. "So you really are a priest."

She pinches her lips between her fingers as she stares at me at my desk. I see her trying to soften me up, make conversation the way she does with Bridget and Daisy and everyone else who comes through our doors. I keep the wall between, standing a good distance away where I belong.

"How can I help you?"

"Bridget sent me. There's a leak at the house in the second floor bathroom."

I let out a groan. "It does that every once in a while. You'll need to replace the seal…"

As I glance up at her, I see that familiar deer-in-headlights expression, and I realize that the possibility of her figuring out how to replace the seal in the tank is about as likely as Misty being able to do it. There are only three hours until service tonight, and if I don't get this thing done, it'll be a mess. I can't improvise. I've learned that before.

"I'm coming," I groan.

"You probably should have hired someone who could fix a toilet."

I give her an impatient glare as she bites back her joke.

"Let's go."

She climbs into the van's driver side and breaks out in laughter. "It's a habit," she says as she stares at the steering wheel. "I keep getting in the passenger side and then remember these dumb cars are backwards."

"Looks like you're driving." I watch as she puts the stick shift in gear after we painstakingly went over it for hours just a few days ago. It gives me a touch of pride. Not to mention it's strangely sexy.

Back at the house, Bridget is on the phone while folding towels as we go up the stairs together.

"Get my toolbelt from the closet." I roll up my sleeves as Cadence jogs down the hall. My eyes won't move from the way her long dark hair hangs across her shoulders while I roll up my sleeves. As she returns with my toolbelt, I nod my head toward her. "Go ahead, put it on."

She answers with a look of annoyance. But she does it anyway. God, I just want to make her mad. I love seeing those feathers ruffled.

With the belt wrapped around her waist, pulling her short shorts even farther down on her hips, I have to ask myself how the fuck I got here. How did this girl land in my lap, learning how to fix a toilet and drive a stick shift, and I tell myself that if I didn't really want her here, I would have found a way to get rid of her by now. I could have told her no, but I didn't. I could have put up more walls between us, but I haven't yet.

"Alright. You need to take the top off the tank and get in there." She gives me another one of those disgusted scowls, but she does it. "Now, flush the water out without letting it fill back up. Then, you're going to have to reach in and remove the worn out valve seal."

She silently gags, and I bite my lip to keep from laughing. I'm sitting on the edge of the tub as she bends over the tank, putting us in very close quarters and that denim-clad rear end of hers on full display. When she gets the broken seal out, she screams and tosses it into the bin.

She may hate every second and make one hell of a mess, but after about an hour, the job is done. Cadence clearly isn't afraid of getting her hands a little dirty, like she's on a mission to prove me wrong. Aside from Misty, I haven't found anything Cadence is actually afraid of.

I find myself wanting to push her boundaries a little more and more just to see how far I can take it. But even I know how dangerous a game like that is. I hear the warnings in my head. I just choose to ignore them.

# Chapter 9

## Cadence

"Cadence, we have a long drive today."

Before he can get a second bang on the door, I fling it open and stare at him with a bright six a.m. smile.

We're driving to Dublin today for an appointment with the consulate to get my replacement passport and apply for my work visa. I'm so excited I hardly slept last night. Until now, this felt like just a wild idea, but now it feels real.

As I take in the man standing in front of me, my excitement about the work visa and trip to Dublin is suddenly washed out by the fact that I haven't really seen Callum in his everyday clothes. He's been in his priest thing and he's been in work clothes, but right now he's standing in front of me in a snug-fitting pair of dark jeans and a T-shirt that makes his biceps look so good I want to gnaw on them like a teething baby.

"Where are you going?" I ask, leaning against the doorframe. "Looking like a snack."

Callum is currently occupied with something on his phone, but his eyebrows jump as he slowly looks up at me, staring at me like I've grown a dick on my forehead. I nearly slap my hand over my mouth. I do not know why I said that. I forgot who I was talking to for a moment. Probably because I'm just excited and in a good mood, but if I've learned anything in that last week and a half it's that my stony-faced housemate does not make jokes.

"Like a what?"

I clear my throat and close my door without looking at him again. "Ready to go?"

I can feel his stare on my face as we descend the stairs in the darkness. Our appointment is this afternoon, and even though it's only a three hour drive, he promised me we could see a little bit of the city before we head back.

The sun is just coming up as we start our drive, and I realize that there are some benefits to not having a phone. With my head propped against my arm, I watch the rolling green landscape and try not to let the lingering "oh my god, what am I doing here?" thoughts disrupt how peaceful this is.

The radio is playing quietly, and I notice the lack of uncomfortable silence between us. Turning my head, I look at Callum again, trying to piece him together. He's impossible to categorize. He's not old, but not young. Not like how I imagined priests to be. He's moral, but not outwardly kind. Good looking without being overtly hot or conceited. And I can't decide if I'd rather fuck him or curl up in his arms like a lapdog.

"Why did you become a priest?" I ask, desperate to fill the silence in the car.

There's not much of a reaction on his face. "It was my calling."

"What does that mean?" I don't know what I'm

59

looking for, but his devotion to that answer has me feeling unsettled. He said it so quickly it was either rehearsed or something he's very, very sure about.

He's silent a moment, staring out at the road until he finally asks, "Do you know what providence means, Cadence?"

For a moment, I'm afraid I'm about to get a religious lecture, but just for curiosity's sake, I answer. "No."

"Simply put, it means that I am fulfilling a purpose I was meant for, that God determined my future, and I am actualizing His plan for me. It means He is in control."

"Like fate?"

"No, not like fate. Like God's plan."

"But how did you know? How did you know His plan for you?"

For the first time, he almost smiles, a tiny lift to the side of his mouth, and it creates a ripple effect across his features, reaching his eyes. "He told me."

"Are you a virgin?" The words slip out of my mouth before I can stop it. My cheeks burn as the air between us goes up in flames of embarrassment.

He reacts with a physical shake of his head like I just threw dirt in his eyes. "You can't just ask people that, Cadence."

"I'm sorry. I forget my filter sometimes, but you have to admit...it's a valid question."

"It's none of your business."

"Well, then don't answer it."

The silence overtakes us, stinking up the car with awkwardness. I shouldn't have said that, but I'm not used to being around people who are so uptight. It's like I need to constantly remind myself that regardless of how filthy his mouth is, he's still a priest, and that's not going to change.

"No."

My spine stiffens. No...he won't answer it? Or no...he's not—

"I'm not a virgin. I didn't take my vows until I was almost thirty. I lived a lot of life in my twenties."

Why is this vision of Callum Moore being a manwhore around Ennis suddenly sending scorching hot butterflies careening through my stomach?

Somehow it makes me feel better, like maybe he's made as many mistakes as me. Maybe he's not so virtuous after all, and he has skeletons in his closet too.

"Oh."

More silence, and this time I can tell he's the one uncomfortable. He keeps shifting in his seat and his hands tighten around the steering wheel with every breath.

"How old are you?" I ask.

"Forty-four."

"No," I snap like a reflex. I took him to be in his late thirties, but not mid forties. He's older than Sunny's husband, but it's a different look of aging.

"Yep," Callum says with a hint of laughter.

"You don't look it."

"Well, how old are you?"

"Twenty-four."

"A baby." He looks at me, his eyes scanning my face before I catch a split second glance to my body, and those fucking butterflies in my stomach are making me want to vomit.

The appointment at the consulate office took place a lot faster and with a lot less fanfare than I expected. I filled out my paperwork, they took my statement, and I turned in my application for a work visa all within our two hour window at the office.

By the time we left, I was starving and in desperate need of something exciting.

He takes me downtown to walk around while he searches something up on his phone. "Where are we going?"

The crowd is thick along the cobblestone roads in this part of the town, and I find myself clutching onto the soft blue cotton of Callum's T-shirt as we work our way through it. "I don't know about you, but I'm starving, so I'm finding us some food."

Finally, we turn onto a quieter, emptier street, and Callum pulls me into a pub with the golden embossed words *The Brazen Head* above the door. It's not much different than the one in town, and there's even a lively band playing as we walk in. He pulls me toward a table in the back and we squeeze in, each of us sitting on opposite sides of the old table.

He catches me looking around in awe, and he leans in. "Depending on who you ask, this is the oldest pub in Ireland."

I'm supposed to be impressed by this, but I'm having trouble getting past the way the word Ireland sounded with his accent, and my eyes won't travel away from his lips.

My back is to the band, and I spin around in my seat to watch them. Suddenly, I feel Callum tapping my arm. With a tight-lipped expression, he nods to the seat next to him. I would be able to see the band better from there.

The booth isn't big, and we are flush against each other in the seat. He leans back, his arm along the back of the booth. We look like a couple, cuddled together, but I don't let my mind dwell on it too much.

We each order a beer when the waitress comes by, and

I send him a smirking glance. Is he really allowed to drink or is he just being rebellious? Pretending to live a different life than the one he's living.

He must notice me looking at him because he leans in, pulling me back until his mouth is close to my ear so I can hear him over the band. A chill travels through my spine, and I breathe in his cologne while he's close. "I'm allowed to drink...if that's what you're thinking."

I lean back, tilting my head to reach up to his ear. It brings our bodies so close I know it's dangerous, but I do it anyway. "They have to let you do that." I laugh. "To make up for the sex you're missing."

The tiny muscles in his jaw clench, and I love how easy it is to rile him up. As I pull away, our cheeks brush and our eyes meet, and I want to get caught in the moment. This thing between us feels like something I can manipulate and play with. I want to see how far I can get him to go, how much I can tease him, make him break his vows. I know that sounds cruel and unfair, but it's the only way I can describe what this is.

For the first time though, I see a hint of regret in his face as he presses his lips together and turns away from me and toward his beer.

"Cadence," he warns me. I don't hear his voice, but I recognize my name on his lips. I'm pushing it too far, and he's scolding me, morphing in and out of this role of man who controls me and man who lets me control him.

When the waitress comes back, we order our lunch and finish our beers. I order a second, but he doesn't. Maybe it's because he's driving back to the coast today, or maybe it's because he has to show me that he's not the partier I see.

His arm is back to the booth behind me after we finish our food and my third beer comes to the table. I should stop drinking, but I'm too busy chasing away feelings I can't control or define.

I don't order a fourth, and when the band stops playing, my ears are ringing in the silence. Callum withdraws his arm from the booth and starts acting weird, keeping his elbows in front of him and his eyes away from me.

"Ready to head back?" I ask when the table is cleared.

He hesitates for a moment, and it takes him a while to answer. Finally, he looks at me. "I guess we should."

Then he knocks my elbow with his, and I find myself resting against his arm. My inhibitions are gone with the beer, so my head falls to his shoulder.

"I can't carry you all the way back to the car." I feel his jaw against my head as he speaks.

"Am I doing the right thing?" I ask. I don't know why that's the question, out of all the questions floating around my brain, that comes out, but I need a moment of Callum's certainty. I think about what he said in the car, about God's plan for him, and I'm desperate for even a touch of his resounding faith.

"What do you mean?"

"Is this my providence? How do I know what God's plan is for me? He doesn't talk to me like He talks to you."

I feel him soften, almost welcoming me against his body as he lifts his arm around me to straighten my slumping form.

"You're just not listening."

"Yeah, I've been told I don't listen."

His chest rumbles softly under my head. Did stone cold Callum just laugh?

"I need God to tell me what to do. All I do is fuck up, and I really shouldn't be in charge of my own life anymore. Is that why you became a priest? For the providence.

Because letting Him make your decisions is easier than making them yourself?"

When he doesn't answer for a few moments, I turn my head to look at him. Our faces are so close together I can see the tiny crows feet around his eyes and the brown flecks in his green irises. Judging by the intensity in his eyes, I'd guess I struck a nerve.

"Do you ever fuck up?" I whisper.

"Yes."

His hand touches my arm, and all three of those beers completely take over, which is why I lean forward, expecting him to lean in too—as if vows were made to be broken and I'm worth throwing everything away for. I want to believe that deep down Callum is a fuck-up like me, like him admitting that means that he's no longer better than me. He's not out of my league or off limits. For a split second, I don't feel so alone.

But instead of leaning in, he pulls away, the magnitude in his gaze searing my flesh. "Cadence." There's that warning again.

What the fuck is wrong with me? Am I so codependent that I need someone—anyone—to kiss me.

"I'm sorry," I mutter, turning my body away from him and wishing the earth would swallow me whole.

"I made a vow." He doesn't say it like I'm being scolded. He's validating his reason for pulling away so I don't feel bad about myself.

"Jesus, calm down, Callum. I'm just drunk, that's all." I jump up and stand, heading toward the door. "Let's go."

The floor sways a little until he takes me by the arm, looping his under mine. As we walk back to the car, through the hordes of tourists, he doesn't take his hand off of my arm, keeping me close and walking straight.

As the crowd thins and I've sobered up enough to walk

without falling, his arm still doesn't move from mine. When we get to the car, he opens my door and puts me in. We don't speak a word during the entire drive home. He must sense my self-deprecation because his hand finds my arm again about halfway home. He strokes my skin from the elbow down, and when I finally get the nerve to look at him, he gives me a soft smile. I think it means he's sorry, but for what, I have no idea.

# Chapter 10

## Cadence

The next three weeks, I focus solely on my job. Sunny sends me a new phone, and Bridget helps me get it set up with a local plan. Having my phone back almost makes me feel human again.

It doesn't do anything to ease the discomfort and awkwardness after the drunk encounter with Callum. Work becomes work, and he goes back to staying at the rectory more often than the house. Our conversations stay safely in the realm of work talk, and I almost never meet his sobering gaze when we are together.

We don't talk about the time I almost kissed him. We don't even get close to talking about it. And honestly, I try not to even let it cross my mind. I don't know what I was thinking. I don't even like Callum. I was purposefully putting myself in the path of rejection, just for fun. What kind of masochistic shit is that?

We are just too different. He's devoted and spiritual, linked to some higher power that makes me feel about two inches tall. Meanwhile, I'm some sort of lost lamb who purposefully ignores sage advice and walks right into trouble around every turn.

Plus I'm not attracted to Callum, not like that. I go for younger, more laidback guys. Trying to kiss him was just a way for me to test my control in the situation, to see how far I could make him sin. It was stupid. And I regret it so much I can't even bear to think about it.

The hotel has been busier these days. It gives me more time in the house with Bridget, helping her clean rooms and cook. Less time in the barn with Callum where working without looking each other in the eye becomes unbearable.

When I come down one afternoon after cleaning the second floor common bathroom, there is a group checking in. They are young, American if I had to guess by their accents. There are three guys and two girls. For a moment, I think of Clint and his friends, and check the girls for signs that they could be victims of the same thing I was. But the guys pay and they all seem pretty familiar with each other. One of the boys, with rusty-hair, tattoos up his arms and neck, and a heavy backpack loaded on his back, finds me with his crystalline eyes as I come down the stairs.

"We do serve dinner as well in the dining room at seven," Bridget says with a chipper smile. She offers dinner to all of the guests. They rarely accept, and the Americans never do. Breakfast is a comfortable quick meal they can take to-go or grab for the road, but dinner is intimate, and I've tried to explain to her that it's just not comfortable for Americans who value their privacy and standoffishness. Still, she tries.

The blue-eyed boy smiles politely at her and gives her a nod, which I know to mean he won't be joining us for Guinness stew tonight.

As I get to the lobby, I smile at the group and grab the duster from behind the counter to take to the dining room. The guy finishes paying and keeps his eyes pinned on me as I move toward the next room.

I should just bite my tongue and move on, but he's too cute with those eyes that look like trouble. He puts pride in his appearance, like a groomed show dog who is a champion of the mating ritual. And I can't fucking help myself. The rest of his group looks paired up, standing to the side and mapping out their plan.

"Welcome to Ennis," I say cheerfully as I pass him through the wide doorway. It's all he needs to approach me.

"You don't sound Irish," he says with a mischievous smile.

"That's because I'm from California."

His eyes light up. "And how did you end up here?"

"Same as you, but I loved it too much to leave."

Judging by his curious smile and slow head nod, he's invested. There's a special moment when you're talking to a guy when you can suddenly tell that he's not leaving this conversation without a number, a kiss, or a plan to see you again.

I did this on purpose. As much as I promised my sister I would be good and focus on myself, I need a distraction from what happened with Callum. This boy is too pretty to pass up.

"Suddenly, I don't think we planned enough time in this town." His teeth are so white, I want to lick them with the tip of my tongue.

"Well, what do you have planned while you're here?"

"Some hiking today, then a pub for some live music tonight."

"Sounds perfect," I answer with a brighter-than-normal smile. "Keep in mind we have supper at seven here, and Bridget makes the best stew you've ever had. Perfect for something after your hike."

I see the way his eyes widen, subtly scoping my face down to my neck and breasts. "Oh, will you be at the dinner?" It's not coy or subtle. We're flirting with each other, and the vibe is real.

"I'm here every night," I answer with a smile.

"You live here too then?"

My heart pitter patters in my chest. I bite my lip. "Third floor."

With a careful nod, he tries to ease back his smile but struggles. His friends call him, and he has a hard time looking away from my face. "I'll see you at dinner…"

"Cadence," I smile.

"I look forward to it, Cadence."

After they leave, I'm filled with a confusing mixture of excitement and shame. I would normally have loved moments like these, the anticipation for what's to come. Meeting someone and every moment of buildup until that first kiss then the excitement in every moment that comes after.

But right now I'm feeling a little disappointed in myself. As I turn back toward the desk, I stare face-to-face with Bridget who is clearly blushing and looking at me like I have a wild secret.

"Make enough stew for our guests," I say as I leave the lobby.

"Oh, I am." She laughs.

When Callum walks through the door that night, the group is already back and the table is lively and full of conversation. Taron, Mr. Tattoos and Frank Sinatra eyes, sits next to me. His attention has been zeroed in on me since he came back with the group.

But as the six-foot holy man in black walks in, I find my eyes suddenly glued to him. I want to see his face when he notices Taron's attention on me. Everyone quiets down as he makes his greeting, but his gaze lingers on me and Taron.

After washing up, he finds his seat between Bridget and Hannah, the bubbly American who I thought was attached to one of the other boys but has made it quite clear that she is not. She immediately pulls him into a conversation, maybe out of politeness. The way she turns toward Bridget less and less seems to suggest she's talking to Callum more because he has those eyes that any girl would be glad to get lost in.

I just want to tell Hannah not to bother talking to Callum like that. She clearly didn't pick up on his occupation because he came in without his collar on.

"So what is there to do around here after dark?" Taron's voice pulls me from my envy-induced eavesdropping.

"There's a great pub down the street. Had a little too much fun there the first night I was here." I laugh, even though I can feel Callum's eyes on me.

"Sounds perfect." Taron leans toward me, placing his hand on the back of my chair. "You'll show us where it is?"

As he finishes the question, our eyes meet, and I'm practically hypnotized by those eyes and long lashes.

"Of course," I answer with a smile.

I don't look up after I pull my stare away from Taron's. I know exactly what I will find if I do...or rather *who* I will find, and I don't need his judgement right now.

After dinner, I help Bridget clean up, and Taron meets me in the lobby. Callum is lingering longer than he normally does, but I wish he'd just leave. Without him constantly watching me and feeling the pressure under his stare, I could have a really good time with Taron.

I know it's not forever, but it's for tonight, and tonight could be really amazing if Callum would just leave. Instead, he approaches the rest of the group and asks where they're going. I watch Hannah's eyes light up when Callum offers to walk them to the pub.

Taron hardly notices anything. Instead, he places his hand at the small of my back and we walk together out the door and down the street. I'm too annoyed with Callum to enjoy the feel of Taron's fingers on my bare skin or the delicious spicy cologne he's wearing.

More than once on the short walk, I catch Callum glaring back at us. I feel like my dad is watching me on a date.

In the pub, we find two tables next to each other and sit down after getting our drinks. The band isn't on yet, so we spend the first hour just talking. Taron doesn't seem interested in group chatter. He keeps turning to me to ask about my life in Ennis and how I got here. He tells me that he's from Modesto, and in an apprenticeship to become a tattoo artist. He bites his lip when he's not talking, and it's driving me crazy, but every moment that I get lost in his beauty, I see the dark green eyes watching me from across the table.

I keep my drinking slow. Last time I pounded back the beers, I tried to makeout with the one guy I'm not allowed to makeout with.

Just before the band starts playing, Taron's hand lands on my bare knee and I don't pull away. Sunny told me to stay away from guys, but she doesn't know how bored I am here and how bad I just need a little attention from the opposite sex.

"You're a priest?" a voice shrieks from the next table. Hannah is staring at Callum with a shocked expression, flavored with a smile.

He nods at her.

"A real priest?" The other two guys in the group are leaning in in shock too.

Taron looks at me for confirmation and I nod. "Yep. He's a real life priest."

I see the blush in Callum's cheeks. Hannah doesn't look any less interested now that she knows this, which doesn't surprise me. That's what women do. We go after the ones we can't have. It's a game to us.

After a moment, I feel Taron's fingers pull me closer as he presses his lips to my ear to whisper so I can hear over the music. "I'm relieved. I thought he must have been your boyfriend with the way he was watching you."

Like the way he's watching me now.

Pulling back, I smile at Taron. "No boyfriend."

It's like a final invitation because he pulls me closer by the arm and presses his soft lips against mine. Once his tongue is in my mouth, right at the table with his friends, I know we're having sex tonight.

And I suddenly feel anxious and restless for it. I need it now. And not in a horny, *fuck me now* sort of way. I need it now because the sooner I get Taron into my system, I can get other guys out. I don't want Clint to be the last guy I fucked. And I don't want Callum to be the last guy I almost kissed.

"You want to head back?" I ask when our lips part.

Taron's eyes go wide and a smile lifts the corners of his lips. "Fuck yeah."

# Chapter 11

## Callum

Who am I to stop her?

When she and the tattooed boy leave together, clearly heading back to the house, I have no right to say anything. Shortly after, I wish the rest of the group well and I avoid the house as best as I can. I take a long walk around town, smoking what's left in my emergency smokes hidden in the flower pot behind the church. I go to my office and try to focus my brain on the quarterly budget and the fundraising proposals. I can't.

The numbers on the sheet aren't enough to steal my mind away from the memory of her smile as he whispered in her ear. The way she whispered in mine just a few weeks ago. And the moment I feel the envy as it crawls up my spine, I stop what I'm doing and I open my bible.

*A heart at peace gives life to the body, but envy rots the bones...*

. . .

I know these words as well as I know my own soul. This is my job, my duty. This vocation gave me direction when nothing else did, and I may not be a perfect priest, but it is up to me to share this infinite wisdom, but how the fuck can I do that now that the doubt has crept its way in.

*Lead us not into temptation but deliver us from evil...*

It feels wrong to ask God for the strength to stay true. My faith is strong enough. But then again, I've never been tempted before. Not like this.

It's not her full lips and round features that claim my thoughts every night. It's the warmth of her laugh and the ease of her conversation. If I'm truly being tested, God didn't just send a beautiful woman, he sent the only one capable of truly waking my dead spirit.

I should sleep in the rectory tonight. It's the only wise decision, but I don't. I wouldn't sleep a wink if I tried. I know I'll feel better once I get back to the house and find her sleeping in her own room alone where she belongs.

As I walk back just past midnight, I think about the envy I felt tonight. The envy for what that kid had but also what he is allowed to have. What if I had turned back toward her with a mischievous smile the way he did when she whispered in my ear? Would we have rushed out of the pub together, excitement on our faces and sex on our minds?

Would one night of indulgent sex have fulfilled me? Offered me what this life does? Purpose, power, and promise.

No. It would have felt good in the moment, but it would be my twenties all over again. A constant chase for that high, only to realize that after twenty different girls in one year, the hole inside of me cannot be filled with something carnal and fleeting.

The house is quiet when I walk in, but I hear something indistinct on the second floor as I pass on my way up to the third. Pausing on the stairs, I glance toward the closed doors. I don't know what rooms this group has been divided into, but there are definitely some guests awake.

It could be the crowd I left at the bar. They must be just getting home and still awake.

Then I hear a moan. It's high-pitched and undeniable.

Clearly a cry of pleasure, and I've come to know that voice anywhere. Pushing the rising envy away again, I keep climbing until I reach the third floor and come face to face with Cadence's open door, empty inside.

Something spoils inside of me. It's the jealousy staining all of the resolve I've just spent the last three hours building. Every ounce of reasoning is gone.

It's replaced with anger. Resentment. An aching desire to discipline.

So instead of going quietly into my room to pray and rest, I turn around and stop at the lounge chairs situated in the small alcove on the second floor. Sitting in the dark, I hear the movement in the room and the sporadic whimpers before it grows silent. This is my penance.

Like a cilice around my waist, I make myself listen to what I can't have. It feels like knives in my stomach, and it only feeds the rage boiling inside of me.

Awful thoughts about Cadence dance through my mind. It's my only defense.

When the door finally opens, and I watch her emerge with her normally silky black hair matted against her head, I wait in the dark for the moment she notices me. There is no post-sex smile on her face. In fact, she's worrying her lip and holding her shoulder sunken forward with shame.

"Jesus Christ, Callum," she hisses in a low whisper.

I don't answer, and for one long moment, we stare at each other, me watching from the shadows like a predator and her fresh from the arms of a complete stranger daring me to say something about it.

Then I spot a change in her expression. Sadness washes over her face as she turns away from me and storms up the stairs.

"Cadence," I call to her as a warning, my voice taking on a tone three octaves lower than normal.

She ignores me as she reaches her room, but I reach a hand out, grabbing her forearm and spinning her so that she's facing me. There is shock in her eyes, but I don't let go of her arm.

"Go to bed, Callum." She tries to yank herself out of my grasp, but I only steer her away from the stairs and closer to her open door so that we're out of earshot of the guests downstairs.

"What the hell is wrong with you?" I snap, my teeth bared and my face within an inch of hers. I stare into her eyes, which are growing more and more heated by the moment. "You can't sleep with the guests, Cadence."

"Oh, please," she says, dismissing me. I feel the anger boiling out, and I know we're about to fight, in the middle of the night over something I'm not allowed to say out loud.

"You're lucky I don't fire you right now. I probably should."

"Fine, then fire me," she spits back, her body pressed against mine. I can feel her tits move with every word. "That's what you really want, isn't it?"

My teeth are clenched as I press myself closer, practically in her room. She doesn't want to know what I really want. I can barely process it myself.

"This isn't about the job. It's about you judging me." I've never seen Cadence so angry. Her face is contorted in frustration, like she's fighting back emotion.

"I'm your boss, Cadence, and these are the rules."

"Well, fuck your rules. You're just being an asshole."

"And you're being a slut." I wish I could say those words slipped out without my control, but that's not true. I've let those words marinate for the last few hours...or weeks. It's the easiest thing to think about someone who wants to give everyone else the thing you want. It's not about me...it's about her.

And I know it's wrong. It was different when I was drunk and barely knew her. I know it makes me the worst fucking priest in the world, and the way her eyes immediately mist over and her lips hang open, my heart splinters. Serving the rage I was feeling does not give me relief.

It gives me regret.

"Fuck. You," she says just before she pushes my foot out of the way and slams the door in my face. I deserved that. I deserve far worse, to be honest.

# Chapter 12

## Callum

Somehow, I sleep like the dead that night. But my words to Cadence are the first thing I hear when I wake up in the morning, like an echo of a bad memory. I fucked up.

The anger I felt has drained away, leaving me feeling rotten and cold.

I called her a slut—again.

I meant it.

I've never been so drunk on jealousy in my life, but I was angry at Cadence. Not that I had any right to be, but I hated the way she gave her body away. I hated that she would not see this guy again after today, and she let someone who would never be as close to her as I was...touch her, taste her, fuck her.

If that's not envy, then I don't know what is.

Sitting up in my bed, my feet flat on the floor, I bow my head and I pray—aggressively. Running the beads of my rosary through my fingers, I get lost in the rhythm of my prayer. It settles my mind, getting lost in the chant as it clears away the fog.

*Hail Mary, Full of Grace, The Lord is with thee. Blessed art thou among women, and blessed is the fruit of thy womb, Jesus. Holy Mary, Mother of God, pray for us sinners now, and at the hour of death. Glory Be to the Father, and to the Son, and to the Holy Spirit.*

The full prayer repeats in my head until it feels as if I'm no longer the one thinking it. I am no longer in control. I am lost to the cadence. This is what I love about my faith, how it runs like water through every moment of doubt or fear.

After nearly an hour, I get off my ass and get dressed, feeling somehow renewed. It's Tuesday, which means I need to tend to the farm today before I focus on tomor-row's Mass. I will have to face her today...all day. And I have no idea how she'll behave.

Part of me hopes she's holding onto her anger and she serves it to me. But another part of me is afraid we will never recover from this. After the incident in Dublin last week and now this, she may never let her guard down with me again. I may never hear her stupid jokes or be on the receiving end of that warm smile.

Probably for the best.

She's not down at breakfast, but it's past nine, which is late around here. Bridget is in a mood too, probably annoyed that her only two staff members took off to the pub to leave her alone in the house last night. I have too much to feel like shit for to start feeling bad for that.

"She's already in the barn," she snaps at me, when she catches me looking for Cadence. Does she know something? Did she hear our fight? Or Cadence's visit to our guest's room?

As I hop into the van, I rifle through the glove box for a hidden pack of smokes. I light up on my way over to the barn, noticing the way the dark clouds roll in from the west, so I pull out the weather app on my phone. Whatever we have to do out in the barn today, we need to do it fast because there's a guster rolling in and won't give us much warning.

I spot movement in the stable as I pull up. Judging by the aggressive way she's raking the stall, she's pissed. I can guarantee I'm the last person she wants to see.

Without a greeting, we make eye contact for a brief second before I head to the back of the barn to pull down the extra hay bales for Misty.

I spend the next hour working tirelessly, my mind running a mile a minute with all the things I'm too scared to say. She's stomping around in the barn, doing her daily chores without complaint and actually completing them well.

A thunder cracks in the sky, practically shaking the walls of the barn, and I spot movement in the sky over the water. Misty starts to grow restless in her stable. When I come out to check on her, I find Cadence standing in her stall, stroking the horse's nose and mumbling gently to her. It's a far cry from the girl who was too afraid to even get close to her six weeks ago.

She stares back at me for a moment, and I hardly recognize her. She normally has bright eyes, glowing skin, a heavy layer of makeup to highlight every perfect feature. Today, there are heavy round bags under her eyes and a steely-cold frown on her face. If I had any hopes she was going to forget about what I said last night, that's gone now.

"Cadence," I say quietly, hoping to start a conversation.

She doesn't look away or fight back so I continue.

"I want to apologize for what I said last—"

"Don't bother," she says, breaking me off. "You were right. I am a slut." Her tone is cold and emotionless, like she's defeated, giving me the final word and accepting that insult as truth. It has me gripping the pitchfork harder between my hands.

"Stop it." I'm not playing with her, and my harsh snap shows it, but she doesn't listen.

"You know, I may be a slut, Callum, but at least I can admit it. At least I own what I am."

There she goes. She's bringing out the weapons now, and I'm desperate to fight.

"Oh yeah? What the fuck is that supposed to mean?"

"It means you're a hypocrite. You're just jealous."

My brow knots together as I toss down the pitchfork in anger. If she wanted to pin these feelings on me, I'm ready for it. "Jealous of what?"

"Jealous of me, Callum. Jealous that I get to live my life. That I don't need God to tell me what to do all the time. I can fuck whoever I want, whenever I want. Meanwhile you're stuck with that stupid collar around your neck because you can't think for yourself." She leaves Misty's side and steps out of the stable toward me. She still has the rake in her hand as she walks into the clearing between the barn and stable.

"I have no regrets, Cadence. Don't attack my position at the church. You know nothing about it."

"I know it's the only way you can get people to listen to you. I heard you at Mass. I know you're a good speaker. But you're nothing without it."

My jaw clenches. The smiling American girl full of

personality and joy is equally as spiteful and cruel as she is happy and fun.

"Cadence," I warn her again.

She steps closer. There is so much pain and rage written on her delicate features that it makes her unrecognizable. "Don't you dare apologize to me. You're not sorry, Callum. You do think I'm a slut. Just admit it. I'm the only one who can call you out on how fake you are!"

Lightning lights up the dark clouds in the distance.

"Get in the barn," I snap, ignoring her words, but she doesn't listen.

"Or maybe you weren't jealous of me at all. Maybe you were jealous of him."

I don't hear her words. All I see is the metal and wood in her hands and the approaching storm. "Cadence, goddammit!" I shout.

I don't take the Lord's name in vain—ever. I don't claim to have a clean mouth by any means, but I don't do that. And the only reason I do it now is to get her attention because even her eyes go wide. "Drop the rake." My voice booms enough to snap her out of her spell.

Just as she drops it, a thunderous crack shakes the barn. It's so loud, my ears ring, and I barely hear Misty screaming from her stall.

I hear Cadence's scream, and I register the strike fast enough to grab her by the wrist and pull her into my arms. Quickly, I take her into the barn and hold her shaking body against me as I look up to inspect the roof.

The lightning rods on the buildings do their job. They keep the lightning from burning everything we own to the ground. We can't help the fact that it's loud as fuck and you never really get used to it.

When my ears stop ringing, I hear her muffled cries. In a daze, I pull her away to check her. The strike didn't hit her. She dropped the rake in time. But she's still shaking like a leaf and tears are flowing down her cheeks.

I yank her body back against mine and stroke her back as she sobs. It's not about the lightning anymore. I can figure that much out myself.

She cries for what feels like an hour but is probably closer to ten minutes. I don't know exactly what it is that's causing the tears. Maybe it's me calling her a slut, or regret over sleeping with that guy. It could be the fear from the lightning or missing home. My guess is a combination of all of these things. Nevertheless, I hold her while she does it.

The feel of her soft body in my hands is something I try to memorize. Her warm breath through my thin shirt. The way she fits with her face against my chest, right where my heart hides. How good her hair smells. How easily I could press my lips against the top of her head.

When she starts to quiet and the clouds finally release the rain, I let the words I'd been holding onto go free.

"You're right. I do hide behind my collar. I do like that people listen to me. Most of the time, I do feel like a fraud, Cadence."

She pulls her tear-soaked face away from my shirt and looks up at me. Her eyes are red-rimmed and swollen, but she never looked more beautiful than she does right now, raw and vulnerable and real.

Her gaze lingers on my face and the silence between us is louder than all of the unspoken words. It's not about what we said to each other but about finally accepting that whether or not we should feel things, we do anyway.

We can accept that everything between us is so intense it's hard to define. This quiet moment changes something.

It changes *everything*.

For any other man, this would be the moment I kiss her. And God help me, I want to.

I want to feel those full lips against mine so bad I'm afraid this desire will haunt me for the rest of my days. I wish she never stepped foot in my hotel because of how badly I want to press my tongue past her lips and feel what it's like inside her. To own her. To please her.

She feels it too, I'm certain of it.

Her lips part. She's waiting for me to make the first move. I see yearning in her softened eyes.

Seconds become heavy, weighted moments until the waiting becomes unbearable, and I look away.

"Let's get back to the house."

Disappointment colors her features as she nods her head and wipes her eyes.

I offer to pull the truck up closer so she doesn't have to get wet, but she declines. I think she wants to feel the rain, as if it could wash away the last thirty minutes. Or thirty days.

The short drive feels long as we sit next to each other wordlessly. I can't go inside. It would be best if I went back to the rectory, sleep there for a while. So I pull up to the front and leave the engine running as she starts to climb out. But I can't let this conversation go, so just before she gets out, I speak up.

"Cadence." She turns around and stares at me, and maybe there's hope in her eyes. Hope that I'll tell her to get back in so we can stay in this quiet bubble where the outside world doesn't matter and vows mean nothing.

"You're right. I was jealous."

I don't look her in the eye as I say it, and I'm sure she's asking herself what or who I'm jealous of, but she'll have to keep wondering because I leave her with that as I drive away.

# Chapter 13

## Cadence

**B**ridget lets me have the rest of the day off. I didn't even tell her anything about what happened, but I also haven't taken a proper day off since I arrived, so after a long hot shower and a fresh pair of clothes, I start to feel refreshed, like the rain and a good cry were enough to cleanse the heavy emotions dragging me down.

The weather clears up by the time I get dressed, and I start walking around town with nowhere in mind. I walk to think about Callum. I think about how badly his words hurt last night. How talking to him feels too much like looking in a mirror, the kind I don't want to see. I think about how cold and harsh he can be.

Then I think about how it felt to be engulfed in his arms, even while I bawled my eyes out. He smelled like tobacco and cotton. And him. He smelled like him.

Less than twenty-four hours after I was naked with Taron, and I'm thinking about another man. But in my defense, I was thinking about Callum before, during, and after every moment with Taron. And I knew he was a drifter, only in my life for a quick moment, and unlike the rest of the guys I find myself with, I didn't picture a future with Taron. I pictured sex, and while we had the sex, I pictured it was someone else towering over me. Someone else's breath in my ear and hands on my body.

When I cried out the loudest, it was because my mind would deceive my body and I would believe for a moment that he was really there, inside me.

After a long, aimless walk, I find myself at the church again. There are voices coming from inside, but it's not a service. As I walk in, I'm met with the vision of Callum holding a baby dressed in white, cradled in his arms. The woman who I presume is the baby's mother snaps pictures while the father stands next to Callum.

My heart swells at the sight. His rough, large hands holding the infant with such tenderness does something to my insides. When he looks up, his eyes meet mine. I'm mixed with warmth and regret as I watch him pass the baby back to its mother. It's like I'm reminded that Callum is a religious man; he doesn't just play the part. He is a man with values, family values, and if he knew the things I'd done in my past...

I know myself well enough to know my aimless walk wasn't for nothing. I came here to be near him in any capacity. But even if he wasn't a priest, he and I would never work. We're too different.

He walks the family to the door and I make a quiet, polite greeting to them as they pass. Then, I make my way into the church, soaking up the calming presence it promises.

Walking down the aisle toward the altar, I stare up at the art and stained glass windows. I wonder what it feels like to be like Callum, to have so much faith in something bigger than yourself. To believe with your whole heart that everything is in God's hands.

I could stand here in this peace and quiet all day, but suddenly, I hear oncoming footsteps, and I freeze when he enters the room. He's in his black button-up and slacks. The white collar around his neck reminds me what I said to him this morning. That he hides behind it because it's the only way he avoids being alone. The regret I feel for saying that is real, but I didn't take it back because it was true.

There's something different about Callum here. He seems more at peace and more comfortable. Less miserable. This truly is where he belongs.

Further proof that I need to just move on and forget about him.

"It's relaxing in here, isn't it?" he murmurs.

Solemnly, I nod. "Mind if I hang out here for a while?"

He answers my question with a question. "Want some tea?"

"Sure," I reply even though I don't even like tea. I just don't have anywhere else to go. I'm drawn to him, and I don't understand why. I could be at Yeager's or in my room bingeing something on Netflix, but I'd rather be here. In a church with the guy who has been nothing but mean to me.

I follow him back to his office. "Have a seat," he says, gesturing to the velvet chaise against the wall. It's soft, like really soft, and so inviting. I can't help but rest my head against the arm and sink into the deep blue pillows. When he walks back in, I jolt upright.

"No, relax. I've slept on that thing so many times. It's like a cloud."

He takes a seat at his desk across the small room, and I let the chaise swallow me up again as I lay back down. The room grows silent as he works and I watch him. My eyes travel around every inch of the room, wondering if he inherited this office with its golden bronze statue of Mary or if he chose it. Pretty soon, it starts to feel comfortable, just being alone and silent together. The only sound is the click-clacking of his keyboard as he types. I notice the way he chews on his bottom lip as he writes, and how the bright computer screen brings out the emerald in his eyes.

After just one yawn, I feel myself drifting. This is the most relaxed I've been since I got here—or possibly ever.

"Cadence?" Callum's voice seeps through my dark and empty dream, but his tone is softer and more gentle than usual. When I peel my eyes open, he's standing over me, all in black covered in warm light.

"We should head back for dinner."

"How long did I sleep?"

"Almost two hours." He reaches a hand down to help me up, and as I slide my palm against his, I register how good it feels to touch him. My mind can't process anything more than that: not the cruel man from last night, or the comforting friend this morning. Just that touching him feels nice.

As we walk back together, I feel like there's a tether between us. The peaceful feeling I felt in the church stays with us. We don't talk, and it's a comfortable silence.

Bridget is busy in the kitchen when we come in. Daisy is setting the table. There are guests today, but they're not joining us for dinner.

Callum goes upstairs, and I help out in the dining room. When he comes back down, he's not in black anymore, and I can't help but feel a little disappointed. He still looks pretty hot in his tight-fitting T-shirt and jeans, but I like the look of him in black and that collar around his neck.

Then he does something he never does at home. He makes himself a drink. I hear the ice clinking in the parlor and a moment later he emerges with a short glass of ice and amber liquid.

I'm looking too much into it. I know I am. Like maybe he's trying to loosen his own rules. Maybe he wants to relax enough to do something stupid. Liquid courage.

I shake my head at him with a smile pressed between my tight lips. He gives me absolutely no response which is the typical Callum response. And it's not good enough for me. Walking over to him, I take the glass and raise it to my lips, keeping my eyes on him as the whiskey attacks my tastebuds.

He almost laughs when I react with a pained expression. The alcohol burns my throat.

As Bridget comes out of the kitchen, I realize we're standing toe-to-toe, and she's looking at us with suspicion, so I step away.

Callum clears his throat. "I'll fix you one, but I'll water it down." Then, he swiftly turns away and walks back to the parlor where the liquor is kept. I still feel Bridget's eyes on me as I help her bring dinner out.

I manage to drink half during dinner, and by the time we're clearing the table, I'm feeling warm and buzzed. Callum is too. I can tell by the fact that he nearly laughs, not once, but twice. It's a low-pitched and gravelly chuckle that comes deep from his chest.

Daisy rolls her eyes at us and goes to her room after everything is cleaned up and put away. Bridget is not far behind her. I'm not ready to go to bed yet. The night feels full of promise. Promise of what, I don't know.

Callum finds me in the parlor alone, and I'm sitting on

the floor in front of the large coffee table. They keep a stack of board games in the bookshelf, and I pull out an old version of Battleship and put it on the table.

"Play with me, preacher man."

He doesn't say anything, just shakes his head and sits on the couch opposite me. He keeps his knees spread and props his elbows on his legs, leaning forward with his glass.

"Need some more?" He gestures to my glass, and I pretend to consider it for a moment before finally nodding. We're playing with fire right now.

I set up the game while he goes to the bar. There's a reflection of him in the dark glass with the rolling waves on the other side. I watch him, the muscles in his back and strands of gray in his light curls. I want to run my fingers along his scalp. I want all the things I can't have.

When he sits back down, he looks down at me with narrowed eyes. There's something on his mind.

"What?"

"Every time I get a hit, you have to drink," he says.

"That sounds like a drinking game." I can't help but laugh. My legs are folded up beneath me, and I realize that I'm feeling nervous. What is happening to me? Just last night I was with Taron, but Callum is acting weird.

"It is a drinking game," he answers.

"Priests can't play drinking games." I have to bite my lip to ease the smile that's threatening to stretch from ear-to-ear.

He leans forward, grabbing his battleships from the box and leveling me with his stare. "Watch me."

Naturally, he kicks my ass in the game. My throat is actually getting used to the whiskey, but the room is starting to sway and I lose the game easily because I keep forgetting what spots I already called. He finishes his drink anyway and laughs at me as I rest against the chair behind me.

"What a lightweight," he mutters with a hint of a smile. I like what the whiskey does to him. For a moment I get lost in the dimples piercing his cheeks and the way his gentle accent attacks my gut with warm sparks. I stare at him from the floor, and I realize that in some sort of way, Callum is already mine.

Not like a sexual, boyfriend way, but he doesn't talk to anyone like he talks to me. Outside of the church, he doesn't talk to anyone at all, and I wonder if anyone else gets the real version of him like I do.

I made a mistake sleeping with Taron. I know that now. Sure, Callum has no ownership over me, but I blatantly disregarded what we have, even if it's not a romantic relationship, and I rubbed it in his face. I don't blame him for his anger now. I still hate that he called me a slut, but what would I have called him if he took another woman home in front of me?

It's only been a month, and already, it feels like there is a tether holding us together. Even if we can't do anything about it.

A month.

Something dawns on me, so I grab my phone and check the time and date.

Holy shit. It's the 23rd.

"Hey Callum…"

"Yes, Cadence…" he mocks.

"Do I still work here?"

His brow knots as he stares down at me, waiting for me to clarify.

"Of course you do."

I jump to my feet with a squeal and raise my arms over my head. "Yes!"

"What the bloody hell has gotten into you?"

"It's over thirty days. My trial is over and I still work here. I did it!"

The sudden pride is overwhelming, and I almost want to cry. In these six weeks, I've learned to care for a horse, drive a stick shift, and fix a toilet. I got a work visa in a foreign country and I haven't seen a pedicure or a shopping center in over a month. I feel like a new person.

Callum shakes his head. "Okay, I guess you got me there. You did it."

I can't help myself, and I throw my arms around his neck. He stands a good head taller than me, so I'm pressed against his body, my face close to his neck. Slowly, I feel his hands wrap around my waist. He squeezes me closer, and something in me breaks.

God may have earned his vows, but I feel what's in this hug, and he's not entirely loyal to the one he gave his life to. He's mine.

# Chapter 14

## Callum

Lying awake that night, I can't stop thinking about that hug. It was the second time I had her in my arms today. Just last night she was with that kid, but something has definitely changed since then. When I held her this morning, it was for comfort. But just now...that hug was loaded.

She was squeezing me around the neck, her breasts pressed up against my chest. I felt her hips on mine and her breath on my neck. Not to mention we hugged for longer than the moment called for. It started as a fun, celebratory hug and turned into an embrace we were both craving.

It didn't satiate my hunger. It only fueled it.

Shortly after, we both climbed the stairs together and split into our separate rooms in the dark hallway. She stumbled as she walked to her room, knocking the doorway with her body before laughing her way to her bed, the door closing behind her.

It's been over an hour, and I can't sleep. Unlike last night when we left things tense and angry, I slept fine. It was like my conscience was happy with me for being angry at her, so it could rest. Tonight, with so much potential in the air, so many ideas running through my head and the reckless feeling that I could do all of the things I want to do, I can't catch a moment of sleep.

Her door creaks.

Slow footsteps trail from her door to the bathroom, and I don't move, waiting to hear the bathroom door close. It is just between our rooms, hers on one side the stairwell and mine on the other.

Those creaky wood floors may be a blessing or a curse.

I keep waiting for the sound of the door closing, but it never comes. She must be standing in the hallway, frozen. Or waiting.

Gently, I stand up from my bed, the floor groaning under my feet. It feels like a response, a call. I know she can hear it. I'm in nothing but my boxers, and it would not be a good idea for her to see me in those, so I pull on a pair of gray joggers quietly and step toward my door.

Her footsteps creak closer.

With my hand on the doorknob, I twist and pull it open. It's the loudest thing I've ever heard.

The hallway is bathed in darkness with just the light from the full moon above shining through the skylight and illuminating her form near the staircase. She's just three steps away from me as I peel the door open to look at her, in nothing but a tiny shirt and her underwear.

There is an invisible line between us, one that we are not supposed to cross. I don't know if it's fading or growing bolder, begging me to cross it all the same.

Cadence is staring back, but she doesn't look as intoxicated as she was earlier. There is clarity in her eyes as she waits for me to do something.

Neither of us speak, but my heart is hammering so hard in my chest that I'm afraid she can hear it in this silence.

She licks her lips, snagging the bottom one between her teeth.

God help me.

"What are you doing up?" It's a whisper so faint, only she could hear it.

"Can't sleep."

I want to believe it's because she's thinking about me.

"Me neither." *Because I'm thinking about you.*

Her gaze roams my face, down my bare chest to my loose pants. It ignites a hunger, and I step toward her, closing the distance until we are standing with only inches between us.

Being closer to her, I notice the slight sway to her stance. The alcohol is still in her system, and maybe that's what's giving her the courage to be here right now. Considering that's the only reason I made myself a glass in the first place, I know it's exactly why I can stand this close to her.

I tell myself I'm not breaking any vows by being here, but that's a lie. Every thought in my head is a sin.

Her fingers land softly on the skin at the center of my chest, and I stop breathing. The invisible line shines brighter than ever. With one single touch, she crosses it.

Suddenly, I can't keep my hands off her, but I'm still holding onto my restraint. So I graze my fingertips along her arms from her shoulders to her elbows, and I watch as the goosebumps erupt in the moonlight.

Her fingers reach my belly button, and my stomach contracts as I fight the urge to start panting. I wonder if she can see my heart pounding as my lungs fight for air. Looking up at me, her touch changes course and glides back up, away from the waistband of my pants. She moves so slowly, I both love it and hate it. It's a delicious torture.

With my fingers still on her arms, I move toward her back, feeling every ridge of her spine as I glide my way down between her shoulder blades, all the way to her lower back, where the ridges soften. She has on a tight tank top that lifts easily at the bottom so I can feel the hollow of her back just before I reach the hem of her thin underwear.

I just want to touch her, to memorize the feel of her body, and there is so much still to explore, but I can't go to bed yet until I know her skin against my lips.

With my fingers still at the base of her spine, I lean down until my mouth hovers just above her shoulder. Her hands wrap around my body now, and I know she wants more. I can feel her desire radiating off her skin, and I feel terrible that I won't be able to give her what she wants. But I'm taking this anyway, this one kiss.

With my lips parted, I press my mouth against the crook of her neck. She lets out a sweet little gasp, and I pull her body closer. Maybe I want her to feel what she's doing to me or maybe I just want the friction against my aching hard-on, but either way, I know what I'm doing is fucked-up.

I said I wanted to feel her against my lips, but now I'm desperate for more, so I sneak my tongue past my lips and steal a taste of her skin, causing her to let out a heavy breath again.

The line has been crossed. Vows were broken, and there is no going back from this. Not fucking her at this point will be near impossible, but it's not too late for me. I have to know when to step away, so I release her neck from my mouth and peel my hands from her back. The absence

Sara Cate

of her body against mine is painful as I put space between us.

She reaches for me and staggers where she stands.

"Go to sleep, Cadence."

Her face morphs into a pained expression, and I feel fucking awful for it, but I'm glad I feel awful. I deserve to feel like shit because I took something for myself and left her feeling like nothing more than a temptation.

And she is so much more than that.

As I turn and walk back to my room, I listen for the sound of her footsteps to her own room. Yes, I want to own her body like I've never wanted to own anyone's before, but I want to own her heart too. And for a man like me, that one is far more dangerous because if I fall in love with this girl, I know there will be no turning back and my life will never be the same.

# Chapter 15

## Cadence

"What do you mean he went to Shannon?" I'm trying to hide my devastation, but it's as clear as day. Bridget is starting to look a little exasperated as she folds sheets on the second floor.

"He had to meet with his parish priest. I thought he would have told you that." I hear the sarcasm in her tone, and she's taunting me with the fact that Callum didn't tell me about this three-day trip of his.

"He didn't mention it," I mutter. "Was it planned?"

"I have no clue, dear. He goes from time to time. For guidance." Her eyes drift up to meet mine. "Spiritual guidance."

Message received. She knows this because of me, because I'm a temptation for him, threatening to ruin his faith, and it grates on my nerves. We are more than that. I know it.

Anger burns through me so I storm out, and I don't stop until I get into the van. After slamming the door shut,

I let out a muffled cry and press my face against the steering wheel.

What if he is beating himself up for what happened last night? We didn't do anything.

We wanted to. That much was clear. I felt how badly he craved it as he pressed his rock hard erection against me. This was nothing like my night with Taron, which was just sex. What I want with Callum is so much more than that.

His fingers on my skin awoke something deep and intense. His touch was meant for my body.

And now he's in Shannon being talked out of everything I know we could have together. He's acting like I'm a vice he has to cure himself of. I'm the mistress, and he's running back to his "wife" to beg for forgiveness.

I let out another cry.

Pulling out my phone, I work on my text again. Out of everything I want to say, none of it seems to convey just how many emotions I'm feeling. So I go with the rawest, realest, thing I can muster. No sugar coating. If he is going to abandon me with this lust alone, I have two very choice words he can chew on while he is getting his much needed "spiritual guidance."

*Fuck you.*

I turn my phone off and toss it on the passenger seat. In a rush, I storm off to the barn to drown my thoughts in work, and for the most part, it works.

. . .

That night, as Bridget and I make our grocery list and clear out the fridge, I can tell something is up with her. She's tossing around casserole dishes like she wants to break them.

"I can finish this by myself if you're not feeling well."

I grew up with a sister. I can read moods like psychic, but with her dramatics, I don't think I have to. Plus, I need to distract myself with someone else's drama for a moment.

"I'm sorry," she groans, stopping at the sink as she plunges her hands in the hot water and starts scrubbing. "I'm just exhausted, that's all. This house has been so much fucking work, Cadence. And do you know...I haven't had a proper day to myself in over a year."

"Oh shit," I stammer, but she quickly cuts me off.

"I shouldn't be complaining about the sudden burst in business. It's great, but this was Teddy's dream. Well, it was *our* dream, but I never would have taken this place from our grandparents if I thought he was going to go get himself killed."

She slams the clean saucepan onto the counter, and I know that had to feel good. I'm standing still as stone across the kitchen when I get an idea.

"You know what we need?"

She looks up at me with her shoulders slumped.

"We need to get drunk. Both of us. Let's go."

It takes some persuasion, but finally I get Bridget to abandon our plan to organize the kitchen and take her down to Yeager's. There are only a couple guests at the hotel, and they're all settled in the rooms for the night. Daisy is in her room with the door closed like she always is. We'll only be right down the road.

The pub is quieter than usual, which means it's still almost full but without a band playing it sounds almost silent. We take our place at the bar and Bridget orders us both a pint and a shot like she does this all the time.

Across the bar, I notice the guys setting up to play, but the accordion player's eyes keep finding their way to where we are sitting.

Bridget turns to me with the shot in her hands. "*Slainte*," we say in unison. Learning the Irish term for cheers was part of my lessons on day one, and it's one of the only things I remember from my night with Clint.

"Okay," she says, slamming her empty shot glass down on the bar. "Tell me everything."

My eyes go wide, and I swallow down the liquid fire, trying to figure out what the hell I'm going to tell her.

"Umm...about what?"

"About that little hottie you hooked up with the other night!"

Jesus, I almost forgot about Taron. And even though he's really the last thing I want to talk about right now, it's better than telling her that I dreamt about her brother's forbidden boner last night.

"You're not mad?" I ask before taking a big drink of my Guinness to wash down the whiskey.

"Nah. I don't care. It's your life, but don't let Callum find out." She laughs. "He's a prude when it comes to that stuff."

I don't bother telling her that Callum doesn't just know I was with Taron. I'm pretty sure he listened in on the whole thing. Or that he called me a slut for the second time that night. But I almost want to correct her about him being a prude. That's not it at all.

Callum lives with so much envy it has turned into resentment. He's devoted his life to the service of the church and he believes so heartily in the cause that he hasn't stopped to think about what he's been giving up for it.

"Okay, okay, I'm serious," she says after another round of shots shows up. "Tell me everything before I drink too much and forget it."

So I tell Bridget everything she wants to know about Taron, how he had tattoos all the way down to his Prince Albert and how he was very attentive to my needs. She loves every minute of it, and it becomes very clear that she hasn't seen any action in a very long time. It's fun, but I don't get the same satisfaction out of the story that I used to.

After a while, the band plays, and we stick around for their whole set. When they finish, the accordion player makes his way over, just as I predicted, and Bridget beams at him like he's made of gold. As I ease myself out of the conversation, I know my absence will go mostly unnoticed, and for a moment I'm almost jealous of her.

She's probably falling for that accordion player right now while the one guy I'm craving is off with a priest trying to pray me away.

# Chapter 16

## Callum

My spiritual guidance is coming in the form of Tullamore Dew.

The pub down the street from my Father Markus's church is just as holy in my eyes. And considering I backed the fuck out before walking in today, I had to find the next best thing.

Her text came two shots in.

*Fuck you.*

I deserve that.

What happened last night scared the shit out of me. My dick wouldn't calm the fuck down for hours after our little hallway rendezvous, even after I gave it what it wanted. Well, not exactly what it wanted, but the closest thing. The thought of her spread out on the bed in front of me, open and begging for me played in my mind as I jacked off three times. It did nothing for my guilty conscience.

It didn't stop me from wanting to break down her door and ignore my vows for one night.

I knew this would happen. I treat my faith like it falls somewhere in the middle of my hierarchy of priorities. The farm comes first. The church. The house. Then my faith. So I'm not surprised that it's falling apart. The first pretty thing with tits and an ass comes in and I crumble.

Shocker.

Cadence deserves better than this. A little space between us for a few days should calm things down. We need clarity. At least, I know I do. I just hope she's getting clarity and not running to the first dick that presents itself while I'm gone.

"I should have known I'd find you here." A deep voice behind me shocks me, and I turn to find Father Markus walk in and take the seat next to me.

Markus is about twenty years older than me, but has been in his priesthood for the same exact time I have. He and I went through seminary together, and he was granted a parish just an hour from mine. He is my mentor in many ways. I used to look up to him, how he could toe the line between well-behaved and spiritual. He drinks with his congregation, sits down with them at dinner, helps them pray, and takes their hand through every moment of their lives. He used to give me so much shit about taking my vows because he was sure that I was too wild to tame.

He raises a hand to the bartender who brings him a Guinness without him even having to ask.

I gave him a heads up this morning that I was coming, and now I guess my plans of cancelling my trip are gone.

"Oh yeah? How did you know that?" I ask.

"You never were the type to face your problems head on."

I guess that's true. Too true.

"How can we be so sure of God's plan?" I ask over my glass of whiskey soaked ice.

He laughs in that hearty way he used to when we would study together, and he was convinced I took everything too seriously. At first, I thought I would hate him. The condescending way he would brush my concerns aside, but as time went on, I started to wonder if Markus wasn't somehow more in tune with God, like they spoke about me behind my back. From then on, I leaned on him for guidance. And for a break. Seminary was exhausting, and for a bitter old sinner like me, I found myself trying to force everything that was meant to come naturally.

Like faith.

"It's called faith, Callum. It's not about following His plan, but asking how you can serve His plan. What part do we play? How do we best serve our flock?"

"Some days I don't think I've served Him at all."

Markus laughs. "Of course you have. If you struggle with your purpose, you must be doing it right."

"How about this?" I ask, turning toward him. "If I can bring one person closer to God, but I have to sin to do it, is it worth it?"

His eyes widen, and he strokes his bare chin with one hand while he thinks. His folded arms rest on his round belly, and I wait patiently for his response.

Father Mark loves ethical questions. It was a constant game while we were in seminary. There was never a clear answer, and rarely a correct one. But each one made me think and understand my value as a man of God. If this is truly what God created me for, then I would be able to answer them with more questions than answers.

"Our souls are not immune, Father Callum. We pay the same penance for our sins, and I would say that if you think sinning is the only way to bring this child of God to salvation, you haven't explored other options yet."

By 'other options', I know he's referring to a chaste relationship and not what my mind wants to consider, which are acts not technically qualifying as sex. I know that is not what he means in the slightest.

After a couple more drinks together, Markus and I walk back to his rectory where he gets me set up for a three-day visit. He wants me to sit in on his service tomorrow and spend my time here praying and being alone with God to find my clarity. I take this to mean we will also be spending time down the street in the pub to find our own clarity, and as much as the idea of being so far from Cadence literally pains me, I know this is exactly what I need. I can be back in Ennis by Sunday for service.

The days go by slower than I thought possible. I never text her back and decide to make the distance real by turning my phone off completely. It doesn't help. While I pray, I tend to get distracted with thoughts of her, missing her and reliving every moment together since she arrived. But by the time I drive back home, I have three truths solidified in my mind:

One: Cadence was sent to me for a reason. And the reason is not for me. It's for her. She came here lost and alone. She is the lamb that wandered from the flock and into danger. It's my job to bring her back to where she needs to be, whether that be closer to God or where God wants her to be.

Two: I cannot touch her like I did that night before I left. For her soul and mine. God is testing me. Not with temptation but with the chance to be the priest I always wanted to be.

Three: I am already in love with her. I confessed this to Markus, and he admitted that he already knew this much without ever having met her. He could see it on my face and claimed that it was bound to happen to me eventually.

It was more of a revelation to me. I have never fallen in love with someone before, but I know this feeling can only be described as love. I am a priest, meant to serve God's creation. And out of all of God's creations, she is by far my favorite.

# Chapter 17

## Cadence

Business at the bed and breakfast has picked up. It's the only thing that keeps me distracted since Callum came back and put more distance between us than when he was a hundred miles away. He doesn't sleep at the house anymore. The moment he walked in the door, it was like he was pretending that the forbidden touch between us didn't happen.

No apology for leaving. No response to my text. The level of comfort between us is just gone. He's been inviting me to church with him, but I can hardly bear to be in the same room as him, let alone go somewhere he is center stage.

Bridget and I have been bonding, staying up with a bottle of wine every night, and it's nice. It makes me miss my sister a little less, although I've been avoiding her calls lately. I don't know if I can lie to Sunny, and I know she'll ask about how I've been doing on this little soul-search adventure I'm on. The only thing I've found is that I don't know how to fall lightly for a man. I give my heart too easily, and I'll probably never have enough faith in myself to break that habit.

We've been checking in so many older couples and families that I've been getting a little bored with the job, but when a group of young Americans comes in a couple weeks after Taron and his friends, I perk up. I need to socialize with someone my own age, and I figure a night out at the pub with guests from back home might lift my spirits.

I'm at the front desk when they arrive. There are three of them, all guys. All handsome with bright smiles and charm in their eyes.

"Welcome to Ennis," I greet them. The strange glance they give each other as they walk in seems a little strange.

"Thanks," the blond one says as he walks up to the counter. "We've heard great things about this place."

"Oh yeah," I answer. "Ennis is beautiful this time of year. Are you guys here for the hiking trails?"

"Uh, yeah. You're American?"

"Yep. I couldn't seem to leave." It's the line I use on everyone who asks. It's starting to feel monotonous. Just as I take their IDs and credit cards, going on and on about how I ended up here and stayed, the front door opens and Callum walks in. He's in his black shirt and collar, and I notice the way he pauses as he takes in the three dashing tourists with my full attention, so I do what any jilted girl would do. I lay into the flirting.

"You guys just missed dinner, but if you're hungry, I can fix you something from the kitchen." I lean forward on the counter, pressing my elbows in to boost up my cleavage, which not one man in the room misses—not even Callum. His jaw clenches.

"That would be amazing, Cadence," says the curly-headed brunette.

"Meet me in the parlor, just around the corner here." I give them each a bright smile as I turn and disappear into the kitchen. They give Callum a strange look before they go into the front room marveling at the view from the grand window.

Callum follows me. "Let me help you."

"No thanks. I've got it. I know how to feed three hungry boys." I give a little shake to my hips and smirk as I say it.

"Very funny," he mumbles. He helps me anyway, and luckily Bridget, who took the rest of the night off to go into town with Fitz, her new accordion-playing boyfriend, left dinner out, so I quickly heat up the beef roast before carrying it out to the parlor with three clean plates. He's right on my heels with the silverware and napkins.

"Oh wow," one of the boys says.

"So what do you have planned while you're here?" I ask, dishing up the food onto each of their plates.

They give each other that mischievous glare again, and I force my smile. I don't know what I'm missing, but I don't pry. "Um...we actually heard some pretty good things about the pub down the street."

"Oh, Yeager's? Yeah, you have to go there. You should be able to catch some live music tonight, too."

Each of the guys takes a seat around one of the small breakfast tables by the window, and I lean against the arm of the couch. Callum is behind the bar making a drink, and I notice the brunette boy's eyes keep drifting back there as if his presence bothers them. I'm sure they're not used to seeing a hot priest mixing a drink at their hotel. I almost make a remark about it when one of the guys adds in, "According to the reviews, you make a great tour guide, Cadence."

My cheeks redden. Behind me, glass clinks hard against the bar. Suddenly, I hear my name on his lips again, and I realize that I never told him my name. All I hear is my breath on every slow inhale and exhale before I finally respond.

"Me?" I have to force my smile as it spreads across my cheeks. Inside my head, I'm screaming, *Not in front of him. Please don't hit on me in front of him.*

"Yeah," the brunette adds with a charming grin. "If you're not too busy, we'd love a tour."

"Well, I don't really give tours, but I'd be happy to walk you guys down to Yeager's."

They all agree amicably, and I can feel Callum behind me, seething. Suddenly, he's sitting at the couch he was at the night we played Battleships, when everything between us was at its best, before it was ruined. He's leaning forward, his elbows on his legs, staring at me like a predator. There is no humor in his eyes, not lust or love. It's something dark and ugly. It's jealousy.

"What about after the pub?" one of the boys says, stealing my attention away from Callum. "Where does the tour end?"

Another one of the guys sniggers, and suddenly holding my smile feels impossible, but I manage to keep my face light. "Um...what exactly was in that review?"

They laugh, and I get a somewhat sincere look out of one of them. Inside, something in me is turning cold as I realize exactly what is happening.

Taron must have let the word spread. I am the Ennis Bed & Breakfast whore. An amenity listed on the website, like a complimentary breakfast.

I couldn't keep my stare off of Callum if I tried, and I do try, but my eyes drift there on their own. It's like I need his stare for comfort. He's waiting to see what I will say.

What will I say?

The old Cadence wouldn't hesitate. A night out with three hot guys, yes. A night *in* with three hot guys, sure.

I would go along with whatever they wanted because that's what I did. Who was I to turn down the attention, mistake it for love and let it devour me.

But now, Callum's hard glare is turning me to ash.

"Let me go get you guys some dessert."

In a rush, I cross the parlor toward the kitchen. I don't even see Callum get up, but the moment I'm alone in the kitchen, he's at my back.

"Tell them no." He's so close, I feel his breath on the back of my neck.

"What do you care?" I ignore him as I pull out the dessert plates and dish out three pieces of pie. "Why should I tell them no?"

He roughly grabs my hips and spins me, pinning me between him and the counter. "You know why."

My heart hammers inside my chest. "No, I don't."

"Yes, you fucking do."

"You've barely spoken to me for two weeks, Callum. You left me without a word. Who's to say you won't do that again? If you want me, you better get the fuck over it, because you don't own me. I can fuck whoever I want."

He snaps, grabbing the hair at the back of my head and pulling down so that my face angles up toward him. It's a stark contrast to the man with the feather-light touch. I may have had Abel already, but now I'm bringing out the Cain, and I like it.

I push away from him, part of me knowing that I'm

113

only getting more heated. The other part can't be this close to him. It's too much, too tempting to fall right back into the routine we had before. One more touch and we'll fall off a cliff we can't climb out of, and I refuse to be a problem for him.

But as much as I fight him, I feel like I would die right now if he let me go.

"You know that's not true, Cadence. I tried to stay away from you. You know as well as I do that I *do* fucking own you."

His hand is still in my hair, and he's so close I feel like I'm drowning in that scent of his I love so much. "I won't stay celibate for you. I won't just turn down every man forever because you have a crush and can't do shit about it."

"So you'll let those assholes fuck you instead? Is that what you want to be, Cadence?"

"Unlike you, Callum, I make my own decisions. I say what I do with *my* body."

"Not anymore," he snaps as he crashes his mouth against mine.

"You can't," I manage to gasp out before his tongue is in my mouth, and I become water, dripping through his fingers. I catch a glimpse of the white square at the collar of his neck just before I open myself to him, and my fighting hands turn into passionate grabs for his shirt and skin.

My senses are flooded with Callum as he squeezes my hip in one hand, the other still buried in my hair. As our mouths move together, I let myself believe that the world inside this kiss is the only one that matters. No vows. No rules.

His hands are on my legs as he lifts me to set me on the

counter, squeezing his body between my knees. Immediately, I feel the hard bulge pressed against me, and I pull him closer. We are going to do this. Finally, he will let down his guard for one night, and I can have this thing that I've wanted for so long.

A voice calls from just outside the kitchen near the front desk. "Cadence?"

Callum breaks the kiss, but I hear him growl a low hum of irritation, and I know it's the way the man called my name like he had any rights to it that pissed Callum off.

"Tell him you're not going," Callum whispers against my mouth.

Our eyes meet and I search for any sign that this is real. If I stay with him, will he make me his? Will Callum be another lost cause in my search for love? My heart can't handle another devastation.

"Tell him." He squeezes the flesh of my hip so tight it starts to hurt.

My hands find Callum's stubbled cheeks, and I let them roam the landscape of his face, a face I've stared at for over two months, wishing I could kiss it and touch it.

"Then what?"

His features soften. He can't answer that question. *Then what* is impossible for him to say at this point.

"Excuse me?" the voice calls again.

"Coming!" I answer, jumping off the counter and pushing past Callum to greet the young man in the lobby.

"The guys are taking our bags upstairs and we were just going to go to that pub for drinks. We'd really love it if you would join us."

I've never walked away from a man I wanted. Never. But tonight, I do it for the future-Cadence who will know the heartache I fear.

"I'm in," I say with a smile.

Callum doesn't stop me as I grab my purse from behind the counter and walk with the guys outside. I leave him to clean up the mess and close up the lobby and parlor, but I catch his face in the window as I walk away.

# Chapter 18

## Callum

She's crazy if she thinks I'm going to sit by and let her disappear into that room with those three guys. I'll let her have her moment of freedom, but I'm still on her lips, and she won't be able to drink away the memory of that kiss.

Fuck, that kiss. It was my first real kiss in over ten years, and I could die happy with that kiss alone. But I want more.

I want to never stop kissing her.

With those full lips against mine and that soft, round ass in my hands, I don't know that there's anywhere else I'd rather be. So while I sit on the second floor, where I sat while she fucked Taron, I let the memory of her mouth against mine fill my time.

I had been doing so well, keeping my hands to myself and sticking to my rules. I let Father Markus's words carry through each day. *I am here to serve God's purpose. It's not up to me to question it. I can save Cadence, but I can't do it by fucking her.*

These were the words that got me through it. But then tonight, seeing those guys trip over themselves trying to win her attention, I threw every one of those thoughts out the window. Right now, my only thought is that I can save her from making a mistake with them.

And that fucking shithead Taron leaving the review, which I found, online.

*The staff was super friendly. Especially Cadence, the American tour guide who not only took us to the pub and partied with us, she gave me a special tour of the bedroom afterward. So accommodating.*

I consider tracking this piece of shit down and making him pay for that, but I settle on deleting the review and making sure Cadence never sees it. Why did she still go out with them after she knew what they wanted from her?

Because she doesn't know her worth, that's why. Cadence gives her heart and her body away in hopes that it will be enough to please them, but she never gets anything in return.

How do I make her see she's worth so much more than what a review says online? How do I make her believe that God loves her? That I love her.

A door opens downstairs, and a single set of footsteps enters the house and heads straight up the stairs. I know it's her when she gets to the second floor, and she stops to stare at me. God I hope nothing happened at the pub. It was a risk I was willing to take to let her go in the first place, to see that I'm giving her space, a choice.

"I don't think we're going to get a good review this time." Her voice is cold and flat, and I'm standing and closing the gap between us just as she puts up her hands.

"No."

Without another word she turns and heads up the stairs, but I'm quick on her tail. Unable to keep my hands off her, I snatch her by the waist and stop her.

"You think this is easy for me?" I spin her so she is facing me. I'm down a couple steps so our faces are almost level with each others'. I hold her by the shoulders, afraid to touch her face because if I do, I won't be able to stop myself from kissing her. "Watching you leave with these guys, wanting you the way I do, knowing you'll give them more than they deserve. What am I supposed to do?"

"Will you fuck me, Callum?" Her tone is so even and casual, the question makes me flinch. My hand goes to her mouth, the other to her lower back. With one small push, she is sitting on the steps, with me between her knees. I lean her back, her elbows on the top step as I rest my body on top of hers.

"Don't ask me that." Slowly, I remove my hand from her mouth.

"Will you?" She gasps, and I see the desire clouding her features. "Will you love me? Devote your life to me? Marry me? No. I know you won't, so why are you doing this? What could possibly come of it?"

"Do you want me to?" I nuzzle my knee higher up so it creates friction between her legs. My lips are so close to hers now.

"Of course I do." Her answer comes out in a light breath.

This time it's her who presses her lips against mine, and I nearly lose myself in the soft movement of her mouth as she runs her tongue across my lips. I let her lead the way, but when she takes my bottom lip between her teeth, I lose myself.

With her body laid out on the stairs, I have her before

me like an offering on the altar. Letting my hands drift up her legs, I feel her tremble when I reach the inside of her thighs where the skin is so soft and plush that I can't help myself and take a quick pinch which makes her jump.

I know what's waiting for me at the top of her legs, and I bide my time, enjoying every second of her body in my hands. She begins to writhe while my lips trail down to her neck, her earlobe, her shoulder.

Not one time do I think that this is wrong. If God is here in this moment, he can't fault me for what I'm about to do because it was my faith that prepared me for it. The unwavering ability to worship something so perfect and all-consuming. To give my very soul to power greater than me. Powerful enough to commit my life to. My mind screams that this is wrong, but my heart doesn't know the difference between God and Cadence.

"Touch me," she breathes into my ear, and I listen, letting my fingers skim the edge of her panties, feeling the moist fabric where her arousal has soaked the cotton. Carefully, I peel back the fabric and run my middle finger along the soaking center. She lets out a heavy exhale as I touch her, exploring every inch.

"You're touching me, Callum," she gasps against my lips as if this moment is too big to not make a mention of it.

I want to do more than touch her. So much more, and my throbbing cock wedged between us won't let either of us forget it. She doesn't move her hands to touch me. Her elbows are still propping her body up against the hard edge of the steps, and maybe that's a good thing. I'm not ready to feel her hands on me, yet.

For now, I'll take what I can get, and I peel her panties aside to plunge one finger inside her, making her cry out a deep moan. My thumb finds the sensitive spot that makes her body jolt as I slide another finger in, stroking them in and out while I watch her face.

Her head hangs back, her lips open and her eyes clenched shut. Her cheeks are tinged pink, and my God, the sounds she's making. I could record them and listen to them every second for the rest of my life. It's exquisite.

Too fucking beautiful to feel bad about.

"Don't stop," she moans, and I pick up speed. I feel like an animal, overcome with lust and greed. The filthy fucking thoughts in my head are anything but righteous.

I'm going to come in my pants, without a doubt. Who wouldn't? Every sense is consumed by the feel of tight pussy in my hands, the sound of her pleasure, the look on her face. If only I could taste her...

I want to put my face between her legs and lap up every ounce of dripping arousal from her body, but I need to take this slow. What I'm doing is wrong, so fucking wrong, and it's not just about the vows I've taken. This is my soul at stake. My relationship with God. My honor as a man.

Of course, every single one of those thoughts goes out the window as her breathing picks up speed and grows more shallow. I know she's close. So I settle for the only taste I can get, and I run my tongue from her clavicle, up her throat and to her lips where I invade her mouth with mine.

Slamming my fingers inside her one last time, I grip her tightly and feel her body explode with her orgasm. Every muscle tightens, and her thighs close on my hand, squeezing them in a vice grip as she stops breathing altogether. I've never seen anything more beautiful in all my life.

It feels like her pleasure lasts forever, and I don't want to take my hand away from this spot, but as she relaxes against the steps, her eyes find mine, and she melts. Reluctantly I pull my hand away, and I let the dirty thoughts take control. With her moisture still on my finger, I run them along her lower lip, remembering the drunk night I touched her bottom lip because I wanted it to be mine.

I steal a kiss, so we can both taste what we've done.

When I finally pull my lips from hers, she reaches for my pants, and I grab her wrist. "No, Cadence."

"But—" she cries, and God help me, I almost give in. But letting her touch me would lead to other things, and I can't break any more vows than I already have. I can't.

I pull her up and fix her skirt, kissing the top of her head like it makes what I just did acceptable. The look on her face as she stares up at me says *now what?* And I have no clue how to answer it. Going to bed together is out of the question.

She reaches up toward me, lifting onto her tip-toes. "So I guess it's goodnight then?"

Relief floods through me. Pressing my lips to hers, I murmur my response. "That's probably a good idea."

I can't stop myself from taking one more deep kiss to fill my dreams and a tight squeeze of her ass to think about while I shamefully relieve myself in my own bed, alone.

She walks quietly back to her room, and I turn toward the bathroom. When I walk inside, I shut the door and turn on the light. The first thing I see sends a wave of guilt to my gut. My reflection in all black and the white collar around my neck. Cadence's arousal is still coating my right hand, and I'm staring at a man who is supposed to be wholly devoted to God and God alone.

It becomes clear as I wash up, unable to look at myself in the mirror that if I continue down this path with Cadence, it will cost me everything I've worked for and lived for. For something that surely won't last, I will sabotage my own soul.

But it's also blatantly clear that I have absolutely no choice in the matter. At this point, I couldn't stay away if I tried.

# Chapter 19

## Cadence

He's avoiding me again. When I wake up the next morning, he's gone. He's not at the barn when I show up to clean Misty's stall, and he doesn't show up to the house for the rest of the day.

I get that this is a moral conundrum for him. I understand that he's torn between his vows and his desires, but I'm not just some vice to avoid. I'm a person, with feelings and needs, and I hate being avoided.

When I mention it to Bridget, how Callum is around less today than normal, she reminds me that it's Wednesday, and he has Mass tonight.

So naturally, I'm feeling the sudden urge to get right with God.

After helping up around the house and turning a couple of the rooms over for new guests checking in tomorrow, I duck out at five and head to the church. I'm a little late, so by the time I walk in, in my simple blue dress with the high neckline that hugs my waist and flares out enough to not be too risqué, I hear Callum's voice the moment I cross the threshold.

He sounds like a different person up there. There is more charisma in his voice while he's preaching and for the short time that I get to watch him without him seeing me, I see just how fit he is for this job. Callum is the best of both worlds. He's just the right amount of young and fresh while also representing the ancient and holy side of the faith. The way he talks, he makes me believe.

He spots me just before I slide into the back pew, and his speech falters. He wasn't expecting me.

Just after finishing his sentence, he takes a moment, turning away from the crowd and walking back to his altar, looking as if he's thinking over his next words. I wonder briefly if he's thinking about me. What we did last night. I squeeze my legs together just reliving it in my mind, the feel of his hand against my thigh, the way he knew exactly how to bring me to climax, the heavy thickness in his pants, grinding against my hip.

He may look like a priest, but I've seen a different side of him. The man behind the collar. It may have been a long time since he's been with a woman, but he's definitely been with enough to know what he's doing, and he may be committed to those vows, but he has some serious desires he can't deny.

I grip the edge of my dress and squeeze it tightly over my thighs. I admire how handsome he is up there. The lights above catch the blond in his waves and bring out the golden tint to his skin. I would have never stopped and had a second look at Callum if he were in Pineridge and we were just two regular people. But now, he's all I can think about. I crave the comfort I feel when I'm around him. The familiarity we've built. The way he makes me think, looks at me when I say something bold, treats me like I belong to him.

Which I realize is a stupid thing to think, but I want him to do more than break those vows. I want him to break them for me. Not just for sex. I want him to break them and make new ones.

Heat pulses in my chest as he continues speaking, and his homily goes past my ears without registering a word he's saying. I'm distracted by the fact that I'm admitting to myself some very serious feelings.

And it's not just that I'm falling for Callum—I fall for men all the time. What's throwing me off about this one is that it feels so different, so consuming, so *real*.

When I look up at him again, our eyes lock. The intensity that burns between us is too powerful to be ignored.

Suddenly, everyone in the pews stands and starts a line toward the front. For a moment, I almost bolt out of the church. I want to run away with all of these crazy feelings swirling around in my brain, but he catches me with his gaze and gestures for me to come up.

I don't even know what I'm getting in line for when I stand behind two young women. They are both fair and beautiful, and I almost get jealous of how long they've probably been coming to this service and hearing his voice.

I watch as each person in the line steps up to Callum, kneels on the bench in front of him and opens their mouths. He places something on each of their tongues and then an altar boy next to him hands each person a small cup of red liquid.

The girls in front of me stare up in adoration as they receive their cracker, and I start to feel incredibly nervous about it when it's my turn.

"Kneel," he says in a low whisper, and my spine tingles with this command. It's something just between us that no one else can hear because no one else knows what it is we have.

"Open." It's the smallest sound out of his mouth, and I almost doubt I heard him say it. Nevertheless, my nipples harden under my dress as I do as he says, holding my mouth open like I saw the others do. I hear him exhale so subtly as he places the cracker on my tongue. My eyes stay locked on his the entire time, and only I can see his pulse quicken.

He mutters a prayer I don't understand and everyone can hear. I don't want to stand from this bench. I want to stay in this spot and stare up at him, doing exactly as he orders me to do. My mind reels with the possibilities, and my body reacts.

I stagger back to my seat and after a few more chanted prayers, the congregation stands and starts to file out of the church. They mingle around the door, and I spot Callum talking to an older couple. He's wringing his hands in a way I've never seen him do before.

His eyes lock with mine, and I hear him excuse himself from the conversation. People seem to be leaving pretty quickly, and I consider leaving too. I hope he sleeps in the house tonight and not here at the rectory.

Suddenly he's at my side, his hand on my elbow. He's ushering me silently out of the main section of the church and toward the hallway where I know his office is. My heart is racing, and it almost feels like I'm in trouble, being marched off to the principal's office.

A moment later we're in his office, and the door behind us is closed. Then I'm in his arms, pressed between his body and the heavy wooden door. We don't speak before his mouth is on mine and his hands are on my hips.

I pour every wild thought in my head into that kiss. Being in this church did things to me, brought out a clarity that is unsettling, and I send every ounce of it out of me through this physical connection between us. He presses his tongue into my mouth, invading me, and I break away long enough to take his lower lip between my teeth. It's like we're at war, each of using these forbidden desires as our weapons.

Then his hands are on my thighs, lifting my dress up and squeezing my ass so tight, I can't hold in the moan, which he quickly covers with his other hand.

"Am I hurting you?" His bright green eyes stare into my soul.

"Yes," I gasp, and he almost loosens his grip as I pull his ear to my lips. "Do it harder."

He lets out a low growl.

I'm not playing fair. I realize that, but I'm competing against God here, and I'll use whatever I have to win him over. I want Callum in ways I've never wanted anyone before, and I'm willing to fight dirty to get him.

"Did you like seeing me on my knees?" I whisper.

He tenses. Then without looking me in the eye, he responds. "You fucking know I did."

With my back still against the door, I let my body slide down to the floor.

"Cadence, what are you doing?" His voice is strained, and I know it's taking a lot to hold himself back.

"What do you think I'm doing?" I answer playfully. "I'm praying." My hands slide to his hips. The look on his face is a mixture of torture and desire. I stare up at him like I did on the bench out in the church, and I know it's breaking his resolve.

Slowly, I start to move the zipper down on his pants. In a rush, he grabs my wrists. "I can't."

I feel momentarily deflated until his hand finds my jaw

and tilts it up to see his eyes. "I want to. God, you should know how much I want to."

"Just hearing you say that turns me on," I reply, and suddenly it's his hands on his zipper and I swallow in anticipation. When his cock springs free, my jaw drops. I was not anticipating this, but a man this size should have never been allowed to join the clergy. He's thick and throbbing, like a dick that hasn't seen a pair of lips in almost a decade would throb.

He strokes it a couple times, and I lean forward to place a kiss on the pink head. He pulls away, and I'm afraid he's about to deny me again.

"Look at me."

My eyes drift up to meet his as he presses it against my lips. The moment his cock touches me, I take control, hungry to taste him. To please him.

I take the base in my hands and run my tongue along the bottom to the top.

"Oh fuck," he moans as he places a hand on the door behind me, caging me in. As my tongue reaches the tip, I stare back up at him as I pull his length into my mouth.

"No. I can't." As fast as it was between my lips it's gone. He pulls away, holding himself in his fist, and I can see him squeezing so tight it looks painful. His face is resting in anguish against his arm, and my heart breaks.

"Callum, it's okay," I whisper, reaching for his hand.

"You could have been stranded at any hotel in Ireland, Cadence. Why did you land at mine? Why did He send you to me if He knew how this would end?"

"Maybe it was providence?"

Still on my knees, I stare up at him, no longer with lust in my eyes, but compassion. I hate this feeling that I'm torturing him. I want to fight for Callum, but I'm not willing to split him in two to do it.

After a moment, he slowly leans his hips back toward me. "Kiss it again."

Eagerly, I oblige, tasting the saltiness of his arousal on my lips. When he relaxes his grip, I take over, holding him in my hand and letting him slide past my tongue.

Every vein in his body pops as he struggles with the pleasure. After coating his dick until it's dripping, I pick up speed, stroking my hand along with my lips. And with my eyes on his, I think about providence. How God sent me here, brought me to this church, to this man, and I try to find an ounce of that doubt I felt before, but it's fading fast.

Callum's breathing stops, and I hear him mumble something unintelligible, ending it with a curse word that definitely takes the Lord's name in vain.

One of his hands holds my hair then drifts down to my cheek as I work his shaft, feeling it tighten as it races closer to climax, and I'm absolutely obsessed with this moment. I want to see him drown in this pleasure, and I want him to stare at me when he comes.

He should know I'm the only one who can make him feel this way.

The hand on my cheek moves to the back of my head as his face grows more pained. I want him to lose control. Fuck me like he wants to. Shove his cock down my throat, but he's holding back.

Just then, his body tenses, and he finally jerks forward, reaching the back of my mouth, and I let out a moan of pleasure. I feel him coating my throat, and I swallow down to see his reaction.

I wait for his smile and a warm look of affection, but he nearly collapses against the door, looking more pained and broken than I expected. He pulls himself out of my mouth and zips up in a hurry, leaving me waiting on the floor. He passes me a tissue and quickly moves to make me stand. Then, he fixes my hair and dotes on me like he owes me something.

"Stop it," I mumble.

"I don't know what came over me."

Before he can turn away again, I grab his face and pull him toward me. "You didn't do anything wrong. I know exactly what came over you, and it's the same thing that's come over me since I got here. We can deny it all we want and pretend we don't know exactly where this is going, or we can accept it. It can't be wrong. It feels too good to be wrong."

There's a look of surprise on his face just before he snatches me up by the waist and pulls me against him. Then he kisses me, no longer invading my mouth, but savoring my lips softly.

Everything about this feels wildly out of control, and I know it should scare me, but I've never been more excited about anything in my life.

# Chapter 20

### Callum

"Are you okay?" she asks, trying to keep up with me, but I can't slow down. My mind is racing. My heart is still trying to beat itself out of my fucking chest, and my legs are just keeping up with the pace. I'm afraid if I stop moving, I'll realize what just happened. As if I could deny it.

Her soft hand hooks around my arm and pulls me back. "What is wrong with you?"

"What do you mean, what's wrong with me?" A couple passes us on the opposite side of the street, and I wave politely before turning Cadence down a quiet alley where they can't hear us. "You think I do stuff like that everyday? You think I'm just going to go on with my life like I didn't just fuck up so royally I could have ruined everything I've worked for?"

She scoffs. "Are the priest police coming for you? What about last night? Was that more okay? You were knuckle-deep in my—"

I press my hand over her mouth and corner her against the brick wall. "Don't you fucking say it." Her eyes are round and full of surprise, but then I feel her relax in my arms, and suddenly I want to relax too. Touching her body has that effect on me.

It softens my resolve. It hardens other things.

My fingers are over her lips, and I try to memorize the way they feel. They were just wrapped around my cock like it was the most normal thing in the world. It definitely was not. It shattered the earth under my feet.

Quickly, I let her go. I have no clue where things could go, so I need to be more careful. "Don't you do that again, you hear me?"

Her eyes widen again, and just as I turn back to resume walking home, she grabs my arm again. "You think this is my fault?"

"I wasn't exactly shoving my dick in your mouth, Cadence."

A loud, offended gasp echoes against the narrow alley-way. I wait for her to slap me, but she doesn't have to. Her hurt expression pains me enough.

"I thought you liked it."

"Of course I fucking liked it, Cadence, but is that what you want from me? Blowjobs behind closed doors? You want to be someone's dirty fucking secret? What happened to the girl who pushed me away last night? You knew then that this could not go anywhere. Remember that?"

"I thought you wanted me," she snaps back, her voice full of more charge than before. I feel myself breaking, my temper rising. Pushing her back against the wall, watching for passersby, I grasp her chin between my fingers. "Of course, I fucking want you, but how long are you going to lure in men with a blowjob and a piece of ass, huh? How long will that last? You think they'll love you after that?"

She shoves against me, and I spot the moisture in her eyes. "Let go of me."

It only makes me more desperate to get through to her, so I hold her tighter, pinning her body against the wall. If anyone saw us, we'd definitely be the talk of the town, and word travels fast around here.

"No," I answer, forcing her to look me in the eye. "Listen to what I'm telling you." Still she doesn't stop with her struggle, so I lay my body against hers, my ear just a breath away from hers. "Yes, I want you, Cadence. I want to fuck you three ways to Sunday. I could lift this pretty dress of yours and have you screaming so loud, the Pope himself would hear you." Finally, she stops fighting me, and I hear the struggle in her breathing.

"I want to tell you every filthy fucking thing I want to do to you, but you're not hearing my point."

I pull her face away and press her nose to mine so our eyes are locked. "Fucking you is the least of what I want to do. Your body is not what makes me want to break my vows."

Silence grows between us, and when I pull away, her mouth is hanging open.

Turning away, I start walking again. I have to adjust myself in my pants from the effect of being so close to her body.

"Callum…" I don't turn around. Eventually, I hear her footsteps as she keeps up her pace next to me.

"I have a lot to think about, Cadence."

"Okay."

"I think it's best we keep our hands to ourselves for now."

I shove my hands in my pockets and feel like a real asshole for what feels like dumping her after she just swallowed down what I unloaded in her mouth.

"I understand."

There's an awkwardness in the air after I just admitted what I admitted, and it's true. Yes, Cadence is beautiful, but it's not her beauty that has me laying in bed sleepless every night.

The rest of the walk is silent, but I feel her calm presence next to me. I want to put my arm around her. Touch her hand, intertwine our fingers, hold her close and talk about our day. My heart is aching for this relationship we can't have.

Glancing over at Cadence as we turn the last corner to the street that leads to the house, I curse myself for what I've started. The wind blows strands of her dark hair into her eyes, and I watch as she lifts her pink-painted fingernails to pull it off of her face. When she misses a strand, I reach over to fix it, and her eyes find mine again.

How the fuck did this happen? How did a girl almost twenty years younger than me convince herself that I was worth her time? How long will this last? I could put her on a plane tomorrow, and she'd find a million guys better suited for her. She'd forget all about me and this crazy moment in her life where she almost convinced a priest to break his vows.

"What now?" she says breathlessly.

"Nothing, Cadence. There is nothing now. We have to walk back into the house and be exactly as we were a month ago."

"What if I can't?" The setting sun catches the hints of green in her dark eyes, flecks I never noticed before.

"That's something you have to decide. If you can't do it, then…"

"Then I have to leave."

A pain stabs me in the chest at those words. The

thought of her leaving feels like suffocating, someone robbing me of my oxygen and making me live like that.

But she's right. It's the only option. So I swallow down the burning in my throat and nod.

"Yes."

There is the most subtle flinch in her eyes at my response. But a second later, she straightens her spine. "Okay. I'll think about it."

Then, she turns and walks toward the house. I'm almost proud of her, my headstrong girl. Too beautiful for her own good. Too fucking tempting for mine.

I follow two steps behind and feel a sense of confidence I shouldn't be feeling. Somehow I know she'll choose to stay, even if it means we can never do what we just did.

Then it hits me...what if I can't. I asked her to decide, assuming that she's the only one who will struggle, but what if she does stay, sleeping next door to me everyday. Is having her voice, her laugh, her smile in my life every day worth the pain it will cause me to never be able to touch her again? Can I live like that?

These are the thoughts that drill my ego as we step into the house, and I'm so distracted that I almost don't hear the new voice in the house. It's a woman's voice. An American woman.

And I wouldn't think much of it if it wasn't for Cadence's gasp as soon as the door closes behind us.

"Oh my God!" she shrieks. My heart hammers in my chest as I stare at the beautiful woman, looking no older than me, standing next to Bridget at the front counter. The two of them are wearing smiles and talking like old friends.

I don't get a chance to ask what the fuck is going on when Cadence runs to the woman's arms. The lady is staring at me with a smile like she knows me but I don't know her.

Cadence pulls away and notices me standing there staring in shock. "Callum, this is my mom!"

I can barely react so I move out of habit, reaching my hand to shake hers when Cadence's mom pulls me in for a hug. "I've heard so much about you!" The embrace is longer than I expect, and when I pull away, she's staring at me affectionately. I don't know what the fuck to say. All the things Cadence and I just said to each other are spinning around in my brain.

Thankfully, Cadence steals the attention off me. "What are you doing here?"

"I wanted to surprise you. I contacted Bridget, and she helped me make the plans."

I can't stop staring at the woman, with her long blonde hair that looks like it's dyed from a darker shade. She has plump cheeks and full lips, and the striking resemblance to Cadence is disarming.

For some reason, seeing Cadence's mom reminds me that—if I were able to date at all—I would be dating women her age. She's a beautiful woman but even if I were a single, available man, she wouldn't be my type. She has a California, tanned-skin, plastic surgery look about her.

"Let's eat, and you two can do some catching up!" Bridget leads the way to the dining room where she has dinner set out already.

They mostly talk about people I don't know, Cadence's sister and her new husband, life in California. I can instantly see where Cadence gets her charisma and ability to speak so enthusiastically. Her mother, Claire, has been rattling on for most of the meal and has hardly asked about Cadence. In fact, it's starting to grate on my nerves so I finally lean my elbows on the table and catch Cadence's eyes across from me.

She's trying to avoid me by averting her gaze, but I kick

her under the table. When her mother finally shuts up for a moment to breathe, I interject. "Well, Bridget has probably told you already, but Cadence is the best employee we've had at the house."

Bridget immediately agrees with a smile and a nod.

The beautiful brunette across from me sobers her expression as she finally pierces me with those dark eyes. "You haven't had any other employees."

"Not true."

"And even if you did, I hardly think my shoveling horse shit and plunging toilets is better than anyone else."

I tap her leg again with mine. "Stop selling yourself short. You do much more than that, and you know it."

Her eyes sparkle, and she bites her lip, suddenly taking interest in what's left of her pork roast.

"Like what?" her mom asks.

Bridget takes the lead on this one. "Oh, she's excellent with the guests. I keep telling Cadence that she should look into hospitality as a career choice. She would be a great hotel manager someday. Our reviews have skyrocketed."

"You didn't tell me that," I direct toward Cadence.

"You've seen the reviews," she answers with a bitten back laugh.

"I mean that you want to be a hotel manager."

"It was Bridget's idea."

"It's a great idea."

Her warm smile as she looks away is enough to keep me happy for the rest of the night. I love that look on her face, with a subtle blush to her cheeks and a determination in her eyes, that version of Cadence could rule the fucking world.

"What Father Callum is not telling you is that he did not want to hire me. Not at all."

My blood pressure spikes when she calls me Father like that. I want to hear her say it while I'm—

No. Can't keep thinking like that.

Shaking the thought away, I look up at her. "I won't deny that, but I'll never forget that first day, how terrified you were of Misty."

Cadence laughs. "Oh my God."

A smile fights against my frown. "And the first time you fixed the second floor toilet. Wait until you see her in that tool belt."

"I bet hotel managers don't have to do that," she answers.

I realize she and I are the only ones talking, and I quickly bite my lip to keep from almost smiling again or saying more. It's so hard to be the right versions of myself around Cadence. I'm not supposed to flirt with her or raise suspicion, but I'm not the stern priest who can't even enjoy a laugh or a joke. How am I supposed to be both of these at once?

When I glance at her mother, she's staring at Cadence as if she is meeting her for the first time. I can only assume working on farms and old homes isn't something she is used to where she is from.

"She's a hard worker," I tell her, and her mouth forms a tight-lipped smile.

As Bridget brings out the pie for dessert, we continue talking about the house and Cadence. Her mother barely talks and just listens.

After dinner, Bridget takes her up to get her situated in her room. It's just me and Cadence in the dining room, and I notice the shy expression on her face. She doesn't have to say anything, but I love the way she's looking at me. It looks like she's making a decision, and it's one I'm going to like.

When we head to bed, Claire catches us in the stairwell as we say our goodbyes. Then she notices the way Cadence and I walk together up the stairs.

"You both sleep up there?"

"There are two staff rooms up here," Cadence answers.

Her mom's eyes watch me with a guarded stare as I finish walking up the stairs. It's like it doesn't matter that I'm a priest or that I'm too old for Cadence. She sees through all of it and knows the thoughts running through my head.

Tonight, we go in our own rooms, but just before she disappears through her door, she glances back at me.

"Goodnight, Father Callum."

Leaning against the doorframe, whispering in the darkness, she looks like a dream—which is exactly what she is. A beautiful dream I don't want to wake up from.

"I like it when you call me that." I say it so quietly no one outside of this hallway could hear it.

"I know you do." With one more lift of her captivating lips, she turns away from me and shuts herself away behind the door.

I can do this, I tell myself. I can be a good priest and love Cadence at the same time. I have to. I don't have a choice.

# Chapter 21

## Cadence

"Please…" I beg, giving him puppy dog eyes and a little pout to my lips. He's still staring down at his laptop, a pile of papers scattered around his desk. Considering it's only been twenty-four hours since I was in his office, and we did things we definitely should not have, I'd say we're acting more normal than I expected.

"Cadence, I have an actual job. I have this budget to approve, homilies to write, proposals to put together. Believe it or not, but this job is more than just showing up on Sunday morning." When he finally looks up at me, a stern expression that transforms into something mischievous, I know he's thinking about last night. Fuck, even with the surprise of my mom showing up, I can't stop thinking about it either. And if it wasn't for that big ultimatum he served afterwards, I would propose we do it again.

He gave me a choice: stay in Ennis and accept that there will never be anything more than friendship or put some distance between us—like an ocean.

I don't need to think about it. I couldn't leave Ennis if I tried, but I'm letting him think there's some deliberation on my part. I want him to worry that I'll leave. I want him to be so afraid of it that he'll do whatever he needs to to keep me.

I want Callum all to myself, and I'm not sorry about it.

"It's just a few hours, and you know the area better than I do. I thought we could take her rental car and see the cliffs. Plus, you know how I hate to drive here. Everything is backward."

His shoulders drop and he gives me a terse glare. "You drive just fine. And you have everything you need on that smart phone of yours."

Finally he stands up and walks closer. It's a dangerous move, and I stare helplessly into his green eyes. I bite my lip to keep from kissing him. If I kiss him, I'll want to touch him. If I touch him, it's all downhill from there. I can't be the one to initiate. That much is obvious now. If he wants me, then he'll have to make the move. It has to be his choice.

He stops just a foot away from me, and crosses his arms. "You don't need me to come."

My eyes devour him with his golden skin, light hair, and high, sculpted cheekbones. If God wanted him to be chaste, he really shouldn't have made him so fucking beautiful.

"I know," I say with a shrug. "I just want you to."

The room falls silent for a moment while we fight the urge to do anything more than stare at each other, and it's difficult. I know he feels the struggle too. So, I send him a simple smirk. "As friends, of course."

He leans forward. "Of course."

"Are we ready?" my mother's voice chimes from down the hall. In a rush, Callum leans away and fidgets in his tight black shirt. It's already warm in this office, and I bet he's sweating bullets in all that snug-fitting black fabric. I want to peel it off of him.

"I'm ready." I turn back to her with a smile.

"Our tour guide is coming, right?" She sends Callum a bright expression, and I see him struggle with his response. He can't deny her when she smiles like that. It's her super-power, and I know this apple didn't fall far from that tree, but the thought of her wooing him with her charm makes my insides twist with jealousy.

"He has to work."

"Give me a few minutes, okay?"

My eyes dart to his face, wide with surprise. He doesn't say anything, but he turns around to settle some papers on his desk. He didn't change his mind for her, I tell myself, but when I turn around I find a victorious expression on her face, and the jealousy twists even tighter.

My mother wouldn't go after a priest, would she?

She wouldn't come to my new home, my new job, and flirt with my boss.

He wouldn't even entertain that idea.

Would he?

An hour or so later, we're standing at the cliffs, and I can't help but feel a little disappointment in my attitude. I was in such a good mood this morning, knowing that I could show my mother around Ennis, hopefully with Callum too. Being with him off work gave me a spring of pleasure.

But he's being distant. When I search for his eye contact, he's too busy being an attentive host to her. He's playing his priest role today. Loving the attention. Loving that someone is rapt with interest at his every word. I see how she leans in over the center console while he talks. I see how she stands so close to him while he goes on and on about the cliffs.

Is he testing me? Showing me what this will feel like if I stay and we continue being just friends? He will never be mine, not really. I can tell myself that he's mine all I want, but as long as I'm around and he's a priest, I will feel like this forever.

The two of them are standing in the grass, looking out over the water, and I'm behind them, feeling as if I'm the one who shouldn't have come. When I look up again, his eyes are on me. The most subtle flinch in his brow shows a hint of worry. But he can't talk to me, not privately. Not intimately.

I want to tell him that my mother is flirting with him, but he probably already knows. It's obvious, but I have no room to talk. I do the same exact thing.

My mother and I have been close my whole life. It was Sunny who she never truly understood. They struggled to maintain a positive relationship her entire life, and there were even violent outbursts that I wish I could erase from my memory. But I love her anyway.

When she turns around and comes over to me, I fake a smile and look out over the water. "Isn't this amazing?" she says, holding her windblown hair out of her face.

"It never gets old."

"You really love it out here, don't you?"

My eyes couldn't avoid drifting to Callum if I tried. "Yes, I do."

"It suits you."

A bursting laugh comes flying out of my laugh. "No, it doesn't."

"Well, okay, it doesn't. But you made it work for you, Cadence. You took a bad situation, and you made it work. You even look happy."

"I am happy, maybe happier than I've ever been."

"Good. You needed this, I think. Since Sunny got married, you just needed a break, and I'm glad you got one. A step away from reality."

My eyes narrow. "This isn't a step away from reality. This is my home."

"For now," she answers with a laugh. "And no, Cadence, this isn't reality. It's a fairytale. Look at this place. It's a long vacation. What are you going to do here? Keep cleaning up horse stables for the rest of your life? Meet a man here? I don't think so."

I don't know why I'm getting so defensive, but my mother's sudden desire to define my experience has me feeling bitter and ready to fight. "I'm not coming back to Pineridge, Mom. This isn't a vacation."

"Cadence, please. What is your plan, then? You can't marry *him*!" She gestures to Callum who is currently standing far enough away and engrossed with something on his phone that he can't hear us. Still, I wish he did hear her. He should hear how unfair that statement is. How unfair all of this is.

"I don't need to marry anyone, Mom. Callum and Bridget and Daisy are my friends, and I love them. My plan..." For some reason, I stutter because it feels like anything I say at this point is cursed. As if I say my intentions out loud, they'll be tarnished with false hope and stupid ideas from a naïve girl. "My plan is to take over the Bed and Breakfast."

Now it's my mom's turn to laugh out loud. This time, Callum does look at us.

"You can't be serious."

"I am serious."

Now, she's angry, and it's coloring the air between us with bitterness.

"You're being stubborn, Cadence. You made a mistake when you trusted that boy, but you don't have anything to prove now. You don't need to stay."

Her words are starting to pierce my conscience, and I'm not feeling as confident as I was a moment ago. This isn't a vacation. I do love it here, but as my mother so subtly reminded me, I fall too easily. I trust too easily. And I make stupid decisions. Is staying a mistake?

Just then, Callum turns toward me and our eyes meet. Quickly, I look away and start to walk back to the car.

I was an idiot to fall for Clint, but until just now I didn't feel like an idiot for falling for Callum. How can I possibly defend whatever this is between us?

"Ready to head back?" Callum meets me by the car, worry written all over his features.

"Yes," I snap.

At dinner, I'm not feeling any better. Even after I spent an hour in my room alone, pretending I was napping, I couldn't shake the feeling my mom's words gave me.

How can I trust my heart if it's made nothing but mistakes?

How much am I willing to let love fool me?

It feels like a sign. Callum gave me a choice, and my mother made mine for me. If I stay, just to be near him, knowing he'll never truly be mine, I'll be leading with my heart, and it will cost me my life.

If I leave, leading with my head, I'll lose him forever, and it will break my heart.

But what future do I have here? Even if I learn to run the B&B myself, will I be doing it for myself or for him?

When I come down for dinner, Callum is in the parlor with my mother. They're sitting at the couch as she leans against him, looking at something on his phone. The jealousy isn't so much a sting anymore as a dull ache, numbed by my new surrender.

"Have a good nap?" she asks, looking up from his phone.

"Yeah." I walk over to the small coffee maker in the kitchen and brew myself a cup. My mother's footsteps close the distance behind me.

"Father Callum was showing me the video from when you two went to Dublin. Looked like fun." The distant memory makes the dull ache worse. That was only a few weeks ago. It feels like a lifetime. The music, the beer, the dancing. The first time we almost kissed. The first time I wanted to. Who was I then? Not the same girl I am now. I was so sure of what I wanted, so excited and determined for this fantasy future that exists only in dreams. I was an idiot.

"Yeah, it was fun."

She grows silent, and I feel the awkward tension returning. "Cadence...I'm sorry for upsetting you earlier. I just want you to be sensible about this..."

"What? Sensible like you? Were you sensible at my age?" I snap back at her.

She flinches. My mother never was and still is not sensible. By my age, she was in love with my dad—or at the very least in love with his money. They married quickly and the honeymoon only lasted a year before they hated each other. Neither one of them honored their commitment, and it was never a secret. I never confronted her about it, but I was too busy holding our family together to care that she had male friends over when Dad was away. Or that she started drinking every day until she couldn't go two hours without a drink. Sunny started retreating into her shell while my mother pulled me out of mine. By the time I was sixteen, I was a fixture at all of her parties. She paraded me around as her best friend. She opened up to me about the men she was seeing, even when she and Dad were still married, and they were my secrets to keep. To her, it was her revenge because he was screwing his secretary anyway.

"I don't want you to make the same mistakes I did, Cadence. Don't rush into anything because your heart is telling you to."

When her eyes dart toward the parlor, my heart skips a single beat. Callum is still staring down at his phone, still out of earshot, and I finally understand that my mother knows. Tears fill my eyes. This isn't about Ireland or the B&B. This is about Callum. About my stupid heart and its recklessness.

Silently, I nod, but it doesn't stop the tears. Suddenly, her arms are around me, and my face is pressed against her shoulder. I want to sob, but I bite it back. Something about crying for another man feels degrading, so I stop myself.

Bridget shuffles into the kitchen, and I pull away in a rush. Turning toward my coffee, I dress it up with the cream and sugar I like, but I feel both of their eyes on me. When we all gather around the table, I know my eyes are still red because Callum won't stop looking at me, and there's an awkwardness in the air.

"Cadence, maybe you'd like to take your mom to Yeager's after dinner?" Bridget suggests, and my spine stiffens. My mother has been sober for almost a year, or so I assume since I haven't seen her in two months. If my mother were still drinking, she'd be so drunk by now that she'd have tried to sleep with Callum right in front of everyone. And when he turned her down, she'd make me take her to the pub to find someone else. She'd be violent,

*Beautiful Sinner*

abrasive, and mean. I've accepted that at least she's trying now.

"I don't think that would be such a good idea," I say.

My mother smiles. "I can handle it, Cadence. I'll be good. I'd love to hear some live music."

My skin boils as I think about my mom in a bar. Sure, it may be a pub here, acceptable for kids and food, but to an American, it's a bar.

"I don't know…"

"I'd be happy to escort the both of you there," Callum says, and I hate my heart for picking up speed.

I'm not comfortable with it, not in the slightest, but what choice do I have? She wants to go, and if she wants to get drunk and ruin all of her progress, that's on her. It won't change anything for me. So reluctantly, I nod my head and agree to it.

But I make a silent plan that when we get home, I'm going to tell Callum that I've made my choice. I'm not staying in Ennis. I'm not willing to stay with him if I can't have him to myself.

149

# Chapter 22

## Callum

Something is off about Cadence. All day she's been acting like she's thinking too much. She was fine this morning when she came into my office, but then after that it was like a switch was flipped. Is she thinking about my ultimatum? That stupid fucking ultimatum that I wish I could take back.

That's not fair. She has a hard enough time making choices for herself, and I just went and asked her to make life choices based on me.

She's sitting across the table with her mom, who is sticking to the ice water while we listen to the band play. It's not the fact that I've heard these guys play over a couple hundred times that keeps me from focusing on the music. Cadence seems to be somewhere else tonight, and I'm desperate to get her alone to talk about it. She's sipping on her Guinness, eyeing her mother nervously every few moments.

Finally, the band takes a break and Cadence's mother

erupts with cheers and whistles. If I can get the band to come over, it's possible I can pull Cadence away for just one moment. I'm not in my collar tonight, not that it makes any difference. Everyone knows who I am.

I wave Roger, the first guitar player over and he answers with a smile.

"Hey, Roger, come meet Cadence's mum."

Claire is on her feet in a second, shaking Roger's hand. He's single and not terrible looking for his age, which is a good ten younger than me—just her type, I bet. It might just be enough to keep her occupied for a moment. The rest of the band makes their way over to make conversation.

Pretty soon it's half the pub and the only chance I have of getting Cadence alone is now long gone. It's when I notice Claire clinging to the twenty-five year old bartender that I realize why Cadence is struggling today. She's watching her mother with a sort of resigned concentration, like she's waiting for the end of a movie she's already seen.

Is that how she sees herself? Is this where she started measuring herself based on how much attention she could get from men?

The heavy third wheel feelings come creeping in around midnight, when Cadence starts flirting back with the guys around the table who do give her attention.

Her Guinness has kicked in, I can tell, and she's starting to look more like the lively, sociable girl I know, but I wish for one fucking second she'd look at me. She's too busy learning how to hold a fiddle on her shoulder or chugging a beer with the guys.

Her smile is fourteen-carat bright, and I've never been more fucking desperate to get her out of here and home, sleeping by herself in the room next to mine. I'm ready to flip this fucking table over.

"It's getting late," I say sternly, leaning across the table.

"Then go home."

Her eyes are playful, but her words sting.

"Come with me."

Now the rest of the table is staring at me.

"I mean, let me walk you home. You shouldn't be walking alone tonight."

"I'll get her home safely, Father Callum." I glare at Michael while the words I want to say to him float through my mind.

*I've heard enough about you to know that's not going to fucking happen*—is what I want to say to the young punk, but I don't.

"You have work tomorrow. I think we should call it a night."

Finally, she looks up at me, and I'm waiting for her to argue when she finally sighs and nods. "Fine. You're right. Mom, are you ready?"

"I guess," Claire replies, and I bite down my disappointment. I want Cadence alone.

Now.

It's just after one in the morning when I finally walk them back up to their rooms. Claire is clearly sober, and she walks just behind us, marveling at every building on the way. Cadence is clinging to my arm in a way that she definitely shouldn't if we are to maintain appearances, but of course, I enjoy it, so I don't pull her off. I am a ball of nerves, ready to let out all of this frustration from today.

When we get to the house, Claire offers to help her daughter to bed, but Cadence brushes her off, claiming that she's perfectly fine, and I don't intervene. As we reach the third floor, I feel Cadence's eyes on me. Sound carries so easily through the house so once we're alone, I'm careful not to make a sound as I scoop her up, wrapping her legs around my body as I carry her to my bedroom.

"What are you doing?" she whispers.

I press her roughly against the wall and shove my face into the crook of her neck. I love the way she smells so much it hurts, but right now her scent carries too much from the pub of beer and other people's breath, so I tear her shirt off her body.

She barely reacts as I pepper her chest and shoulders with kisses. I don't know what I'm doing. I'm breaking my own rules, but I am driven by something much more powerful than rules.

Her hands dig into my hair as I work my way up to her lips. When I finally taste her mouth, my mind goes blank. I have no commitments or vows. I am nothing more than an extension of her.

My hands squeeze her hips tighter as I grind myself against her hard, letting her feel the extent of my arousal.

"Cadence," I mutter quietly, my voice nothing more than a low growl. "I want you."

"No," she argues without pushing me away. Instead she tilts her hips so I grind myself against the exact spot I want to enter her.

"Tell me you're mine," I mumble as I pull down the strap of her bra and press my teeth gently around the soft flesh there. She moans quietly.

"No, Callum."

We're both drunk. That much registers now as we both fumble helplessly toward something neither of us have the mental capacity to stop.

"Tell me you're staying. Say it, Cadence." My hips press her so roughly against the wall, I know it must be uncomfortable for her, but she doesn't protest. She just pulls my lips to hers and kisses me instead of answering my request.

While our lips are still touching, she softly answers, "No."

In my head, I'm telling myself that if I can just get her clothes off, if I can just show her how good it will feel to be naked against my body, to have me inside her, trembling in my hands, then she will change her mind and I can keep her.

I have a momentary vision of us years down the road, still secretly fucking in this room and nothing will be ruined. No one will be hurt. We will be happy and everything will be fine. If I were still somewhat sober, I would stop myself, but I'm not—so I don't.

With her body still trapped between mine and the wall, I begin to fumble with the button of her jeans, and she doesn't stop me. Instead she almost seems despondent, kissing me like it would be more painful not to. When I finally have her pants undone, I pull them to the floor, letting her fumble with taking them off completely while I work on my own.

We are breathless and there is an eerie silence that surrounds our panting. When I hear a subtle creak in the distance, I ignore it because Cadence is standing in front of me, completely naked and ready to be mine. All mine.

Spinning her around, she lets out a whimper as I face her toward the wall and press her shoulders forward. This carnal, needy part of my brain takes over, and it wants nothing but to take, take, take.

Grabbing her hips, I pull her back toward me, and I hear her whisper my name. It sounds like a plea, and I don't know if it's to stop or keep going. With one hand on her hip and the other working to pull my pants down, I hear another creak.

We both freeze. I'm inches away from having her, from a place there is no going back from.

"Cadence?" a voice calls from the end of the dark hallway. Cadence and I move like lightning, breaking apart and trying to cover our bodies. We are no longer silent or graceful.

"What's going on?" her mother calls as she steps closer. I pray it's dark enough that she didn't just see her daughter naked and bent over at the hands of a priest.

Bile rises in my throat. What have I done?

"I'm fine," Cadence calls back, her voice cracking. She rushes out of view of my open door. She's still naked, but struggling to pull her jeans up.

"Father Callum?"

I wince, swallowing down the lump in my throat.

I've never hated myself more than I do at this moment.

"Yes?" I try to make my voice sound deeper and more authoritative as if that makes any fucking difference at this point.

Cadence brushes past me as soon as she is mostly dressed and goes to her room, stopping at her open door. "Goodnight, Mom," she mutters before slamming it closed.

My skin burns hot as Claire's eyes focus on me through the dark space. She's not angry, but there's something sad in her expression.

"I'm sorry." Why I say it, I don't know. Maybe because it's the only thing I feel at this moment. I could be saying it to Claire or to God, but it doesn't change how strongly I feel it.

"You two drank too much tonight."

She says it like it's a proper excuse. It's not, so I can't respond.

"Goodnight, Claire." Softly, I close the door just before I hear her walk down the stairs.

I escape out of the house early the next morning. Sticking around for breakfast doesn't sound like the best idea, and even if it makes me feel like a coward for running off, I do actually have work to catch up on at the church.

My phone sits silently next to me on the desk, and I can't exactly be surprised. Why would she talk to me at all today? She clearly tried to shut me down last night, and I didn't listen. She didn't stop anything we were about to do, but why would she? I was the one who was supposed to be showing restraint. Last night, I had none.

I'm halfway done with my proposal I'd been meaning to write for six weeks when a gentle knock on my door pulls me away from my laptop.

Claire is standing in my doorway with a pensive expression on her face. My stomach drops. This is not a conversation I want to have, not here.

"Good morning," she says with a fake smile. "I brought you some breakfast since you left so early."

Subtle dig.

"Thank you." I keep my tone professional as I stand up to take the foil-wrapped plate from her hands.

"Mind if I come in?" she asks, helping herself to the chair in front of my desk. There is a bronze statuette of the Virgin Mary just behind her, and I keep my eyes on it as I close my door and take my seat across from her. I can't look Cadence's mother in the eye.

"Claire, I'd like to apologize—"

"Please don't. Let me just talk for a moment. I didn't come for your apology. If I've learned anything through this recovery it's that apologies do nothing to erase or right past mistakes."

My eyebrows spike and I lean back in my chair. How many times have I said this same thing to my congregation? How many times did I lead them into the confessional with the belief that asking for forgiveness does not erase our sins but opens our hearts to God so that we may choose better in the future?

"I wasn't a very good mother, Father Callum. I was too harsh on my youngest and too open with my oldest. I raised Cadence like she was my friend, and I'm afraid that no one truly guided her like I should have."

This is not how I expect her to start.

"What she got from me was a mother with too many regrets and a drinking problem. What I got was a perfect daughter who cleaned up my messes and took care of me and her sister because that's what Cadence does. She takes care of people. She gives without asking for anything in return. She looks for love in all the wrong places and she gives her heart too easily."

My jaw clenches and I have to swallow down the emotion building in my throat. I already know all of this, and she knows it. She knows I know that falling in love with Cadence was the worst thing I could do to her, and if she's trying to make me feel like shit for it, she shouldn't bother. I already do.

"I'm asking you to be careful, Father Callum. Be careful with my daughter."

"I—"

"She's in love with you."

Her words stop the beating heart in my chest. "I promise it was just a drunk night, Claire. It's not like that."

"I know my daughter, Callum. She's in love with you, and it's not about what happened last night. She'll stay

Sara Cate

here for you and wait forever if you ask her to. She'll give you everything you want."

I feel sweat start to bead on my forehead. Either I've been avoiding this acceptance that things were serious with Cadence or I'm learning it for the first time.

"Cadence and I are just friends, Claire. I regret what happened last night, but I'm forbidden from having a relationship of that nature with anyone. Cadence knows this."

"She's a rule breaker, Father. Are you?"

This woman has a lot of guts to ask me this stuff, but she is the woman who raised Cadence, so it only makes sense now.

"I take my vows seriously," I answer astutely, sitting tall with my arms on the desk. Inside I'm shrinking.

"I'm sure you do," she says as she stands up and walks toward the door. Just before she disappears down the hallway, she turns to me and adds, "The devil's in the details, you know."

Oh, don't I fucking know.

# Chapter 23

## Cadence

**B**ridget chose to come with me to take my mom to the airport in Shannon a week after she arrived. We never talked about what happened when she caught me with Callum that night after the pub. He also never came back to the house after that. Not even to eat. Not even to work.

I tried to put him out of my mind, but as I help my mom with her luggage at the airport, I feel her unspoken words in the last few minutes we have together. On one hand, I hate that her harsh conversation about my flippant decision to stay ruined most of her visit. I just haven't felt like myself since. All I can think is that no matter what I choose will be the wrong decision. How do you follow your heart when you can't trust it?

Bridget stays in the car while I walk my mother in. We have a few moments, so we sit down to have a quick cup of coffee, and I feel her hand reach for mine over the cafe table in the airport.

159

"Relax, baby."

My eyes lift to find hers, and I shrug off her words like they have no impact. "I'm fine."

"Cadence, I've known you for twenty-four years. I've never seen you so confused in my life."

A heavy sigh releases in my chest. "I just feel like I can't stop fucking up."

She does something I don't expect. She laughs. "Oh, Cadence. Everyone fucks up. Especially at twenty-four."

"I don't want to come home." I force the words out because I'm afraid she'll be disappointed by them.

"Then don't."

"Am I stupid for staying for him?" Tears start to prick around the edges of my eyes, and I have to clench my teeth to stop them from falling.

"No, but I want to see you do something for yourself, Cadence. You're always doing so much for others. You spent your whole childhood taking care of me and your sister. Your relationship with men has always been about meeting their expectations, but what about yours? If you stay for him, what is he going to do for you?"

A few minutes pass in silence while I let her words sink in. Then, they make a call over the loudspeaker for her flight, and we both stand.

As I hug my mother goodbye, she squeezes me tighter than normal and whispers in my ear, "I love you."

On the drive back to the house, my mind continues reeling, thinking about what my mother said, about taking what I want in life without thinking what other people want. When was the last time I took something for myself? I went on this trip in the first place for myself, didn't I?

It was the first time in my life that my sister and my

Beautiful Sinner

mother didn't need me. Sunny was off in honeymoon bliss and Mom had just gotten out of rehab, finally standing on her own two feet. No one needed me. I remember the exact moment that I panicked and did the first insane thing I could think of. I booked a trip across Europe, and I was so desperate to be something to somebody, I was practically an open target for Clint and his friends. They made themselves rich on my insecurities, and now I'm afraid I'm doing the same thing all over again.

Is Callum taking advantage of me? Is this thing between us what he wants or what I want?

My heart answers with a deafening thump: this is what *I* want. I want him so bad, more than I've wanted anyone. So much sometimes I feel like I could die from this wanting.

I want that oozing confidence of his when he's talking about God behind the altar, offering me a world I never thought was available to me. I want the deep tone and the sweet accent in his voice. I want those emerald eyes to be mine.

And I want his body. I want to live in the quiet world we create when we touch, finding pleasure in each other's bodies. We haven't even had sex, and I know that he has ruined me for other men. With one touch, he made me his.

For so long I've chased boys who seemed like the pretty package, and I never bothered to look deeper. It's not about Callum's looks; it's the way he looks at me that makes my stomach flutter and my toes curl. He challenges me, gives me confidence, shows me what I can really do, and never doubts me.

I want him. There is no question, no doubt, not anymore.

When we get back to the house, I check for him again, but his room remains untouched and empty like the last six

161

days. We didn't have any check-ins today, but we have a full house tomorrow, so we both get to work prepping the rooms and the food. It's a grueling work day, and neither of us talk much. I can tell that Callum's absence is weighing on Bridget too, but she doesn't dare ask me about it. Maybe it's too uncomfortable. Maybe she's mad at me. I can't tell, and I don't bother asking.

It's past midnight by the time I call it a night and head upstairs. After a hot shower to wash off the sweat and weight of the day—hell, the whole week, I walk back to my room in my pajamas. I don't even make it to my bed before I realize that I can't do this anymore. There is no fucking way I'm going to crawl into my bed and wake up in another day without expressing the thoughts that have been screaming in my head.

Tonight, I feel the conviction, but tomorrow it could be gone. Slipping on my work boots, I tip-toe out of the house. Walking in the dead of night in nothing but my skimpy PJ shorts and tank top was a dumb idea. People spill out from the pubs as I walk, and I hear their calls, but I ignore them.

What the hell am I doing? How the fuck did I get here? Chasing after the man I love into a church and not a bar?

When I reach the church, shivering from the chilly night air, I realize that I have no fucking clue where his rectory is. I've only ever been in the front entrance and his office in the back. I figure there's no better place to go than in, so I pull open the heavy doors and am suddenly greeted by dim candlelight and eerie silence.

My heavy boots scuff against the floor echoing through the church as I walk down the aisle toward the empty pews. There's something about this place and the feeling I get whenever I'm inside. It's an overwhelming feeling of being alone and not alone at the same time. At peace, safe, comfortable.

This is my competition. This is what Callum loves about this place, about God, about everything he's willing to give me up for. How can I possibly compete with this? Me? The girl with a body count too embarrassing to even utter, the queen of mistakes, the girl who was once so popular for all the wrong reasons. I've committed sins Callum doesn't even know about, sins he may never be able to overlook. How could I possibly ask him to give any of this up for me?

Suddenly, I find myself sitting in the pew, and before I know it, I'm praying. I've never prayed before, so I'm probably not even doing it right, but I whisper to God as if he can hear me.

"How do I compete with You? If providence is real, then You brought me here for a reason. Am I being punished? Is this my penance for what I did? Even if it is, I'm not going to just give up. I know what I'm up against, and I'm willing to fight for him. I thought I loved so many men before, but it never felt like this. And now I think he feels the same about me, and what if he's the only one who ever will. You can't blame me for fighting for this."

I don't know how long I sit there before a light comes on from down the hallway.

"Cadence?" He's standing on the other side of the room in a black T-shirt and black pants. His hair is disheveled, and there are heavy bags under his eyes. He looks like shit, and for some reason it makes me happy to see it. My heart nearly bursts at the sight of him.

Quickly, I stand. All of the words that I had prepared for this moment have vaporized in his presence. Judging by the look on his face, he doesn't want to speak either.

In just a few long strides, he's standing right in front of

me, and I barely have a moment to register anything before his lips are on mine. The kiss is ravenous and desperate. It's vindication. It's everything we've been hiding and torturing ourselves with for so long.

His lips devour me, trailing down to my neck, my shoulder. His moans are hungry and soon they turn into words. "I'm sorry," he mutters over and over as he worships my body with his mouth.

Instead of melting under his touch, I meet his passion, and kiss him back with every ounce of fight I have in me. I can hardly breathe as he picks me up, wrapping my legs around his waist. The world tips and turns and I don't know which way is up until I see the ceiling and realize I'm on my back on the stone floor. It would be cold if my body wasn't suddenly made of fire.

Every fiber of my being needs him, and I recognize the same need in him. Desperately, I pull up the fabric of his shirt and he shrugs out of it quickly. His soft skin in my hands makes me want to weep. My fingers cascade across the muscles in his arms and around his shoulders.

"I need you," I whisper to him as I lift my mouth to his chest.

"I'm here," he answers, taking my lips with his.

My shirt comes off and next my shorts so that I am bare on the floor for him. The only thing between us are his pants, so I break the kiss and look him in the eyes. I don't need to say a word because he knows. I won't reach for his pants. I won't be the one who makes that move. It has to be his choice, and he does not hesitate.

The sound of his buckle clinking in the silence of this midnight mass will be a sound stored in my memory forever. It is the moment he lets himself go in the current pulling us both away. It tore me from shore a long time ago, but now it's his turn.

He sits up to pull his pants down, and then it's just us. Our naked bodies on the floor, no longer guided by lust but by something stronger.

I feel the head of him against my core, and I hold my breath, my eyes not leaving his. He enters me with a force that makes me gasp and want to scream. Once he's buried inside of me, we melt together. My legs wrap around him and his spine curls around me, his head buried in my neck. For a moment we stay still, enjoying this first bonding our bodies, like it's some ancient ritual.

He groans into my skin, and I know the Callum that holds back and plays it safe is gone. The Callum I know, the one who takes and commands and doesn't apologize is about to take over, and my body pulses in anticipation.

Sitting up he looks down at me, pressing one long kiss on my lips just before he rears back and slams into me again. This time I can't hold back the cry that slips out.

He does it again and again, keeping his eyes on me the whole time. I don't bother keeping it quiet anymore. When he pulls my leg over his shoulder, I almost fall apart. My moans of pleasure vibrate across the walls of this church set to the perfect rhythm of his heavy grunts.

His hands grab my hips as he rockets his body against me, building speed and momentum. My back slides against the floor, and he yanks me back, slamming himself even deeper.

I grab helplessly onto his arms as my body teases me with a climax. It's like I'm overwhelmed with every sensation that when his fingers find my clit through the frenzy of it all, it breaks down the wall between us.

"Come for me, baby," he growls, and I do. I am shattered into pieces on the floor, in more bliss than I ever thought possible. My cries are muffled by his mouth as he crashes his body onto mine, losing himself in his own orgasm, his cock pulsing inside me.

I don't stop kissing him, and he doesn't stop kissing me.

When he finally does pull out, it feels like the first time my body has been without his in a lifetime. Like him fucking me was the most natural thing in the world.

"Let's not speak yet, okay?" he whispers against my mouth, and I nod. I know exactly what he's asking, and I feel the same way. Tonight we just want to be together. We don't have to work through anything or worry. We can just be us, as we are.

I wake up to his movements in the bed before the sunrise. He's sitting up with his feet on the floor, and I can barely make out his form in the darkness.

A nervous feeling slides through my body as I wake. What if he regrets what we did? He's already retreating away from me. I reach for him, my fingers a breeze on his back.

When he turns toward me, I can make out the familiar cold expression on his face. "I didn't mean to wake you."

"Where are you going?" When I hear myself, all of my internal cautions start going off at the same time. *Don't be needy, Cadence. Don't start acting like you do with all the guys. This one is different.*

He quiets my worries when he lays back down and presses his lips to my forehead. "I thought I could sneak back to the house and get you some clothes so you don't have to go home in whatever that was."

"They're called pajamas." I cuddle my body against his as his arms envelope me.

"I think I'd call them knickers and certainly not something you should have been walking around town in at one o'clock in the morning."

I laugh with my face pressed against his chest. "Knickers."

"You think that's funny?" He gently pinches my side and I squirm, laughing harder until our limbs are tangled, and I feel him growing more and more aroused against my body.

We did it two more times last night after running back to his rectory, which to my surprise, looks a lot like a bachelor pad. No decorations, no fancy furniture. There's not even a TV. Just a small kitchen, an even smaller bathroom, and a bed.

Before I know it, our gentle laughter turns into heavy breathing and I'm on my stomach. I hum into his pillow as he kisses every vertebrae down my back. When he lifts my hips, I'm already wet for him and he slides in easily. We groan in unison.

This feeling of being one with him is enough for me. Before Callum, sex was something I did to please whoever I was with. It was what they wanted of me. But with Callum, it's so much more. It's pleasure and connection. It's rough and beautiful.

My hands grip the bed sheets as I wait for him to take over. I've already memorized his rhythm.

With a tight hold of my hips, he fucks me hard until I'm practically lifted off the bed and coming with the force. Just as my climax hits, he lifts my body so I'm flush against him and he pinches my clit until I'm splintered in two, undone with ecstasy.

We collapse together on the mattress. He pulls me onto his chest as the morning sun starts to creep into the space through the two small windows. It gently illuminates the golden cross hanging on the wall across the room.

"Do you feel bad?" I whisper. We haven't spoken much at all since I showed up last night, and with the new day dawning outside, it feels impossible to avoid the difficult conversations.

He shifts uncomfortably. "No. Do you?"

I laugh. "Why would I feel bad? I'm not married to God."

With a scoff, he shakes his head. "It's not like that, Cadence."

I love hearing his voice again, our stubborn conversations, and mostly I just want this back, this friendly back and forth we used to enjoy before everything got so heavy.

"What's it like then?"

"It's more like a commitment to serve my congregation. I'm bound to this church because it's my calling. It's not about sex, really. It's about devotion. I can't devote myself to anything or anyone else because this is my duty."

When he describes it, I find myself even more attracted to him. Callum doesn't do anything with half of his heart. He serves with everything he has, and knowing I get a sliver of that passion fulfills me.

But that one part doesn't sit well with me. He can't devote himself to anything *or anyone* else. It stings.

"I'm not asking you to devote yourself to me." It hurts to say it, but it's true. I want any part of him, even if it's not all of him.

His eyes find mine, and there's a hint of remorse in them. His lips flinch like he's holding back something he wants to say.

"It's not fair of me to ask for your devotion, Cadence. I can't ask you to stay."

"I'm staying." Even as my answer comes out, I realize it's the most sure I've ever been. "No one meant for this to happen, Callum. You have a responsibility here, and I don't want to take that away from you, so I'll stay. I'll take as much of you as you have to spare, but my heart won't let me go back to Pineridge."

His fingers softly brush the hair out of my face as he pulls his face down to mine. When his lips brush against mine, I feel like my heart is about to burst out of my chest.

What my mom said was true; I do give too much to others, but she doesn't understand that this is what I want. More than anything in the world, I want to give myself to someone who makes me feel loved. Callum does that. I've made mistakes in the past, and I know what they feel like. This doesn't feel like a mistake. It feels like providence.

# Chapter 24

## Cadence

I almost find the hard work gratifying. I kind of love feeling the sweat drip down my back, like I earned it. Luckily, the weather has cooled down in the past few days and it's not as unbearable out here in the barn. I almost like it more than working in the house now.

Today, I take my time. Checking and cleaning Misty's hooves a little longer than usual, brushing her, feeding her. I have enough to occupy my mind as I work. Callum joining me in the shower this morning plays on a loop in my mind, and not just the part where he bent me over and we had to fuck quietly so Bridget wouldn't hear. But also the mundane moments, like scrubbing the shampoo through his hair and watching him wrap the towel around his waist after we got out. Who knew an act so simple could be so sexy?

When I hear the van pull up outside, my mouth lifts at the corners no matter how hard I try to hold it back. It's been two weeks since that night in the church, and I feel myself slipping down a muddy hill with no chance of stopping. I can't get enough of him, and judging by the way he actually *almost* smiles around me, I know the feeling is mutual.

I don't move from Misty's stall as he stalks into the enclosed space. He comes up behind me and pulls me back with force, making my toes curl when he lands his warm mouth on my neck.

"I think it's about time you went for a ride," he mumbles against my neck.

"I went for a ride twice last night and once this morning" I tease, reaching back to run my hands through his thick hair.

He lets out that deep chuckle that is Callum's version of a hearty laugh. "I was talking about the horse."

I freeze. "Ride Misty?"

"Sure, why not?"

I can't help but laugh, pulling him toward the hay bales in the barn, and out of sight of Misty. I'm not sure I can do it in front of a horse, especially her. She always looks so much smarter than I thought animals were supposed to look.

"Because I've never ridden a horse before. What if I fall off?" I shove him onto the stacked bales and climb over him straddling myself over his body. Leaning down, I place a kiss on his lips.

"I won't let you fall off," he mutters while I'm kissing him. Our kiss turns heated, and I feel myself slipping again, like I literally can't get enough of the feel of his stubbled face against my lips. I fumble for his buckle while he works on my jeans. In a rush, I climb out of them as he frees himself from his pants.

As I settle myself on him and find my rhythm moving with him inside me, I stare into his eyes. There is no tomorrow or the next day, at least no future worth thinking about if I can't have this. Once we crossed the forbidden line and gave into whatever this is, it's like we both went all in. He didn't bother acting like he regretted it or felt bad. That first time on the floor wasn't even the last time we did it in the church.

If he can give into this so easily, maybe he can let it go completely. Maybe once he realizes I'm enough for him, he'll choose me.

I keep up my grinding. Just thinking about him being mine sends me over the edge. I clutch his chest and he pierces his fingers into the flesh of my hips as he drives my body until he's filling me up again.

Collapsing against his chest, I inhale his scent and kiss his chin.

"You feel warm," he mumbles, running his hands up and down my body.

"Well you have that effect on me." He doesn't respond, which I know to mean that I'm making a joke out of something that Callum is taking seriously. I lift my chin and look into his eyes.

"I'm fine. I've been outside all day, that's all."

I watch as his jaw clenches, and I have to admit, seeing him so worried about me is a major turn on. When was the last time a guy was worried about me?

*He's mine. All mine.*

I lie to myself because, in this moment, it feels possible.

Landing a rough smack on my bare ass, he kisses the top of my head and says, "Okay, then. You're riding that horse."

"Today?" Carefully, I climb off of him and pull up my underwear, knowing that I'm going to have to change them, again, once I get back to the house.

"Yes, today. Let's go."

I stand back and watch as he dresses Misty up in her saddle. Then he puts a hand out for me to come closer, and I feel my heart rate rising with my nerves. I'd much rather watch him ride than get on myself.

Still, when he puts a hand out for me as I put my foot in the stirrup, his calming presence and commanding tone settles some of my worry. "You'll be fine, Cadence."

Climbing on top of the horse requires more grace than I expected. It takes me a couple of tries before I can get my leg over and once I'm up there, I start to panic. It feels too high and I don't have enough control over her.

Callum has her on a lead as he guides her out of the stall and toward the field. He shows me everything from how to steer her and stop her and make her run, but I don't start feeling any more comfortable.

Once he senses my discomfort, he stops the horse and touches my leg. "Look at me."

When I do, I nearly fall into those green eyes. His hand strokes my thigh with such a comforting touch that it's hard to associate him with the same man who probably left bruises on my hips just a few minutes ago.

Either Callum has split personalities or he's very good at playing the necessary part.

"Relax, Cadence. You're in control. I'm here, but you don't need me."

"Don't leave." I feel like a child learning to ride without training wheels. He smirks, then claps my hand.

"I'm not going to leave you."

Holding Misty's reins, I let his words sink in. I'm in control. I am in control.

After a while, I start to get comfortable. His instructions helped, but once I got a feel for controlling the horse, I knew I could handle it. We walk Misty around the yard for another hour before we head back toward the barn.

Callum indulges me when I ask to see him ride her just once around the pen, and I make sure to store that mental snapshot at the forefront of my memory bank. I want that picture of him, snug jeans and long-sleeve shirt on those broad shoulders as he rides against the setting sun, etched into my mind forever.

Once we put Misty away, we ride toward the house, and I'm hit with a sudden wave of exhaustion. I slump against the seat and nearly fall asleep on the short drive over. It must be from the whirlwind of the past two weeks. I don't sleep much, and I've been working harder than ever.

Callum shakes me awake when we get to the house just before I feel his hand on my head. "Jesus, Cadence. You're burning up."

Then it's like it all crashes on me at once. My head starts pounding, my body aches, and my throat feels like I swallowed rocks.

"Straight to bed," he commands as I shuffle inside.

Bridget is staring at us with concern as I bypass the lobby and head straight up the stairs. "She's pale as a ghost," she cries.

"Grab her something to bring this fever down," Callum says in his deep authoritative tone while he's helping me to bed. I can walk perfectly fine. A minute ago I was riding a horse—not to mention him before that, but Callum is acting like I'm suddenly incapable of basic functions.

So sue me if I savor it, letting him help me out of my clothes and into my pajamas. He dotes on me like I'm his child...or his wife. After putting me to bed, he brings me water, two aspirins, and a cold washcloth for my forehead. Then, he doesn't leave.

Taking a seat in the chair on the other side of my room, he watches me drink down the water. "I'm fine, Callum," I admit. "It's probably just a cold. You really shouldn't spoil me."

He leans forward, placing his elbows on his knees and watching me with his cold, calculating stare that I've learned to love so much. "I want to."

My heart still manages to thrum a little faster even though my head feels like it's covered in fog. "You know what they say about feeding feral cats. They'll never leave."

"Good," he replies.

I rest my head against the pillow and fight with the covers. I'm suddenly trembling and burning up at the same time. Sleep starts to pull at me the moment I'm lying down, but I keep my eyes open so I can enjoy this view for a moment longer.

Callum is sitting in my room, not for sex but for me. My thoughts stop making sense as I let that image of him on the horse fill my mind as I drift off to sleep.

# Chapter 25

## Cadence

I sleep away the next twelve hours and barely leave the bed for most of the next day. Callum almost never leaves, except to bring me tea, soup, and fresh tissue boxes when I go through two with my head full of congestion.

"I don't want you to see me like this," I whine, trying to only blow my nose when I know he's out of earshot. "Please leave."

"Not a chance." He refills my water and takes my temperature, again. I overheard him and Bridget arguing this morning when he demanded they take me to the hospital, to which she insisted it was just a cold. I was not dying. He was disgruntled, to say the least.

When I wake up from my afternoon nap, he's sitting in the chair again with his laptop on the table next to him and the Bible in his lap. "You're not being very discreet, Callum. Bridget will start to suspect..." My voice is scratchy, but my throat aches a little less now. I'd like to keep the sultry way it sounds though.

"I don't care," he answers without looking up.

"What are you working on?"

"Tomorrow's homily." Bent over his laptop with the table-side lamp giving him a warm glow, I admire the fact that Callum has all the best qualities of a man approaching middle age. There are faint lines peeking out from the corners of his eyes, and his hands don't have the flawless look of a young man's. His hair is still thick though, even though the light brings out the gray strands along his hairline.

His body doesn't show his age, that much is true. And neither does his libido. On his good days, he can go three rounds, and I've known twenty-year-olds who couldn't pull that off. Maybe it's the twelve years of celibacy that retained his sex drive.

My head isn't throbbing so much anymore and the chills have subsided, so I sit myself up against the pillow and pull my legs out from under the covers. Just thinking about pre-priesthood Callum has me feeling antsy with curiosity.

"What were you like when you were my age?"

His eyes cast up toward me, but his brow line tenses at my words. We never really talk about the age thing. I guess it's eclipsed by the priest thing.

"Your age?"

A smile creeps across my face. "That was twenty years ago, Callum."

He rolls his eyes as he closes his Bible and sets it next to his laptop. "I'm aware how long ago it was."

I tug my bottom lip between my teeth. "So, tell me. What were you like?"

After a heavy sigh and a long moment of contempla-

177

tion, he relents. "I was lost. Reckless. Like I was always in search of something but never satisfied."

"Were you religious?"

"No. Not really. My family only went to church when we really had to. Bridget and I sort of abandoned that when we moved out. But when I turned twenty-eight, I knew I needed to do something with my life. So I started going to church, hoping God could answer my questions. Give me the guidance I needed. The first time I prayed, as an adult man, I became addicted. When I told my family I was going to seminary school, they were appalled. Thought I was throwing my life away."

I keep my comments to myself as I watch him across the warmly lit room. How would I feel if someone told me that? I'd be disappointed too. It feels so final.

"Then Teddy went and got himself killed, and I think they wanted me to drop out. It only fueled the fire. I was determined to do both: run the house and the church, so I spent the next fifteen years of my life working so much that I didn't have time to focus on what I was missing."

Suddenly it's like I can see Callum so much more clearly. The broody, stoic man who barely takes time to smile, gave his life away. He doesn't seem to regret it, but hearing that I have to wonder. Is it really his pride that keeps him tied to his job? The inability to accept defeat or that he made a mistake.

I want to tell him that he may have needed guidance then, but he doesn't now.

"How are you feeling?" he asks when the room grows heavy with silence.

"A little better. I need a shower. I feel disgusting."

He quickly stands and moves toward me on the bed. In absolute horror, I back away as he reaches a hand out for me to take. "Stay away, Callum. I'm too gross!"

"Don't be ridiculous."

"I'm serious. I probably reek, and my whole face is all swollen and congested. This dim light is about all I can handle you seeing me in. Bright bathroom light is out of the question."

He completely ignores everything I say as he flips back the covers and scoops me into his arms. I don't bother fighting with him because it's not worth the ruckus we would cause, and I'm sure Bridget is suspicious enough. But still, I tighten myself into a ball as he carries, hoping that I can somehow mask any odors I've accrued from being in a bed for thirty-six hours straight with a burning fever.

"You're impossible," I mumble.

As we get into the bathroom, he sets me on the counter and shuts both of us in. I desperately hope he's not going to try anything because I don't know if I could turn him down. When I turn around and catch a glimpse of myself in the mirror, I'm mortified. Any makeup I did have on is now smeared down my cheeks. My nose is red and puffy, and my eyes have heavy, dark circles. I look like hot garbage.

I can hardly stand the idea of any man seeing me like this, let alone the one I currently like the most. I've been known to apply a full face of makeup at two in the morning after a promising text message with an invitation to come over and "chill." The only people who see me like this are Sunny and my mom. But the way Callum barely seems fazed has me feeling suddenly very warm and fuzzy, and not in a fever sort of way.

He watches me undress with too much mischief in his eye, but at least he has the decency to let me wash myself up—and shave the important stuff—before he climbs in to join me.

Sara Cate

"So what about you?" he asks as he turns his back to the shower stream.

"What was I like twenty years ago?" I reply with a smile. "You sure you want to know?"

Instead of laughing at me, he pinches my side. I let out a raspy squeal, so he lets up.

"You didn't let me finish. Where do you see yourself when you're my age?"

The laughter in me dies as I try to formulate an easy answer to that question. Do I go with honesty or something fake? I figure if I can be honest with anyone, it's with him, so I swallow down the pain rising in my throat—not from my cold, and I stare at his chest to avoid his eyes.

"I want kids."

The only sound is the shower stream for a moment before he runs a hand from the back of my head to my lower back. "How many kids do you want?"

His voice sounds strained, like it hurts to even ask that.

"A lot," I answer, looking up at him. "Or just one. I don't care."

He gives me that signature Callum smile that only seems to really register in his eyes.

"I know what you're thinking," I say, pulling away to squeeze shampoo into my hands. "You didn't expect me to say that. I don't exactly give off the mom vibes. "

He doesn't respond as I reach up to lather his hair with soap, dying to just run it through my fingers. His hands land on my hips, but I keep my face away from his. Even in the shower, I'm not about to let him kiss me.

"It didn't surprise me at all. I think you'll be a great mom."

As he leans his head back to rinse out the shampoo, I swallow down the lump in my throat. I should tell him,

180

right now. I should come clean and tell him everything. He'd understand. He'd listen and be loving to me about it.

Or it could ruin this perfect moment. And every perfect moment to come.

A moment later, he wraps his hands around my legs and hoists me up. My back is against the wall as I bury my face in his neck.

"Thank you," I whisper.

We don't say another word about it, letting all of those regrets and what-ifs swim down the drain, along with one of my precious opportunities to come clean. As he enters me, my stress melts away. Our good days feel numbered, especially when he brings up the future. So I need to enjoy the ones we have before they're gone.

# Chapter 26

## Callum

There is no normal now. Normal was a bleak chapter in my life when I thought I had everything I needed. Then Cadence careened in and shuffled up everything.

Now we exist in this new definition of normal, and it's ours. I sleep at the house every night, and ironically, I'm feeling more connected and revived at the church than ever before. My homilies come with ease. The scripture speaks to me in new ways I never realized were possible; as if, for the first time, I am hearing a language I didn't know I could speak.

Every spare moment is stolen by her. Kissing her in the barn every morning until I can hardly breathe, sneaking her away into my office after Mass so I can fuck her with my collar on because it drives her crazy. Each night we take turns crawling into each others' beds, and even when there is no sex, I'm still just happy having her close, knowing she's mine. Living in bliss on this side of that

Beautiful Sinner

forbidden line we crossed.

I keep my job up at the church, and she continues killing it at the house. Bridget can't stop talking about how good she's doing, how much she thinks Cadence should start thinking about her future, take some classes, consider a business of her own.

We don't talk about the future, not anymore. That conversation in the shower came at me like a punch in the face. I don't know what I was expecting her to say, but it wasn't that. I thought she'd talk about the hotel or opening her own. But kids…

It's really not so surprising now that I think about it. Cadence would be an amazing mother. It's the giver in her, the selfless nurturer who is always putting others first. I've seen her with the little guests that occasionally come through, the way she plays with them in the parlor, pulling out the board games or running around the yard. Like it's the most natural thing in the world.

But hearing her say she wants kids puts a thorn in the crown of our relationship. And it suddenly feels like it's hanging around as a constant reminder that we have an expiration date.

And it may be coming a lot sooner than I expected.

Cadence and I share a bathroom, one which I barely used before since I liked to get ready for work at the rectory. But since everything has been uprooted, I find myself showering and rushing in the morning to get to the church. Without a toothbrush, I start to rifle through the drawers hoping Bridget stocked extras.

The small drawers are mostly full of Cadence's makeup, hair things and whatnot, but it's a little pink disk that catches my attention. It's not the fact that she owns birth control that shakes up my whole fucking morning—I mean, it's a good fucking thing she does, regardless of my

183

religion's outdated views on the stuff—but my curiosity gets the best of me, and I open it.

The good news is that according to the dates on the package, she's taking it.

The bad news is that she's almost out.

Is it any of my fucking business how or when she takes it? Absolutely not. I took that risk on my own, but it feels a little like opening Schrödinger's birth control pack. I didn't know before today how long we had until we had left to be reckless, but now that I know, my head is spinning.

Last week's conversation put these thoughts in my head. It's making me see things I definitely should not be seeing, especially after one fucking month together—in a very forbidden, extremely secret relationship.

But still...the vision of her with a rounded belly, full with my child…

My brain is all kinds of fucked up today.

Even at the church, sitting with the morning bible study, I can't stop thinking about it. The young mother whose baby I just christened two months ago is nuzzled against her chest. I imagine it's Cadence and a tiny dark-haired infant with green eyes and full lips.

I never thought about children before, and I'm almost forty-five fucking years old. It's bad enough I'm asking Cadence to keep whatever this is between us a secret. It's a whole other level of fucked up to ask her to put off her dreams of a child...or to raise one alone.

"Father Callum." I lift my head from the blank stare I'm holding over the sleeping baby.

Every member of the group is staring at me, waiting for an answer to their question, a question I didn't even hear.

Looking back down at the scripture, I find the passage highlighted for today's reading and manage to pull some bullshit out of thin air. It seems to be enough because the congregation looks happy. The woman with the daughter smiles and nods.

The group lingers around for coffee and donuts like they usually do, and I spot movement by the front door. Just then, my phone vibrates in my pocket, and I open it up to find a picture of bare legs just below a very short skirt, spread wide over my desk.

*Cadence: Forgive me father, for I have sinned.*

Jesus Christ.

I clear my throat and pocket my phone. How the fuck am I going to get these people out of here? They're busy talking to each other, and it's mostly just the keeping up town gossip and boring small talk with a few of the retired farmers. They wouldn't even notice if I was gone, so I make busy work as if I'm cleaning up and need to tend to something important.

A moment later, I'm stalking down the hallway, but instead of being in my office where she was supposed to be hiding, she's coming out of the ladies bathroom.

"Oh hello, Father," she says coyly, and I suddenly don't give a shit that twelve to fifteen of my congregation are standing around the corner, only fifteen yards away. I press her body against the wall and reach up her skirt to palm her warm cunt.

Her eyes pop open and she tries to push away. "What are you doing?" she mouths. She looks at the corner cautiously, waiting for someone to burst in and see us. Honestly, so am I, but I don't give a fuck.

I pull her panties aside and slip a finger in, absorbing the sound of her muffled moans against my chest.

"Callum, stop," she gasps, but she doesn't complain as I begin to circle her clit with my finger. She clings to my arm, and I watch her face change with every movement of my hand under her skirt.

Voices come closer, and we can hear their conversations clearly. They stop just beyond the hallway, caught in another meaningless diatribe, but I know our time is short, so I hurry my progress on her soaking sex in my hands.

She presses against me, caught between the desire to come and the need to flee.

"Come all over my hand," I whisper in her ear, and her jaw hangs open like she's fighting for breath. I'm striking hard now, slipping in a second digit as she writhes. My heavy dick grinds against her just as the conversation outside stops. Any moment, someone will round that corner and see me finger banging my young American employee. The secret will be out, and we won't have to hide anymore.

But then again, I know it's this filthy thing we're doing that makes her seize up in my hands, biting back her cries as she soaks my hand. I love the way her thighs clench together as she comes, a vice grip on my wrist like she never wants me to pull it away. We're both high on the forbiddenness of it.

Just as the footsteps approach, she shoves me away and disappears into the bathroom. I force my hands into my pockets as Bonnie Yeager, the pub owner's wife and volunteer in charge of our bible study treasury looks up from her clipboard.

"Oh, Father Callum," she says with a smile. "I just need your signature on these purchase orders."

I smile at her and try to keep her eyes on my face so

Beautiful Sinner

she doesn't notice the way my pants are fighting against my painful erection. Taking the clipboard, I send her a forced smile.

"Did you enjoy today's discussion?"

"Always. And it felt so appropriate this week. Sometimes the Lord answers the questions we didn't even know we were asking. Isn't that right?"

After signing my name, I nod along. "Yes, He does."

At that moment, Cadence walks out of the bathroom, and I see how Bonnie smiles at her with a little less sincerity as she does with me. Then her eyes travel to her short skirt before returning to my face.

"Hello," Cadence declares cheerfully and looking so natural I'm impressed.

Bonnie returns the cordial greeting, and we all stand there awkwardly before Cadence finally looks at me and says, "Father Callum, I'm sorry to bother you at work. I need the keys to the van to pick up the groceries for the house."

My little actress looks too perfect as she speaks, her hands behind her back and staring at me like I'm her boss and nothing more.

"Oh, of course." I pat my pockets, pretending I've misplaced them. "They're in my office." Then I turn to the older woman. "Have a blessed day, Mrs. Yeager. Thank you for taking care of these forms."

"Thank you, Father Callum." She beams at me with no word toward Cadence as she turns and leaves. As we walk to the office, we listen for her footsteps and the sound of the big door closing before I shut Cadence in my office. I'm not done with her yet.

But as I reach for her, she swats me away.

"What the fuck is wrong with you?" For the first time I

notice the blush to her cheeks and the smeared lipstick she tried to fix in the bathroom.

"What are you talking about?"

"Do you realize what would have happened if we were caught?"

"I am very aware of what would happen." I cross my arms and lean against my desk. I feel a fight brewing between us, and I can't tell if I love it or hate it. She doesn't shy away from arguing with me, but at the same time, it's impossible to get anything through to this girl. She's all talk but doesn't listen.

"No, I don't think you are, Callum. So let me tell you."

I try to reach for her hand, just to touch her while I can, but she pulls away again. "Do you think you'll be blamed for anything? Do you think for one second this town would condemn their perfect priest? Why would they, when they can place all the blame on the new, young American girl who swooped in and tempted you to sin?"

I can't help but smirk at her. "You did though, didn't you?"

"That's not funny." This time she lets me pull her body closer. "I would be a villain, Callum. They would make it miserable for me to stay."

"I wouldn't let them." I press my forehead against hers and steal her lips.

"I think you want to get caught," she murmurs as I squeeze her soft body in my hands.

"So what if I do?"

"What would happen to us?" She asks the one question that turns our back and forth play into a serious conversation about the future, the off-limits stuff.

I pull away and take her face in my hands. "I honestly don't know."

There's something about her questions that have me

wondering if her real question is: would I leave the church for her? Would I marry her if I could? Would I choose her over everything else?

It's a lot. Too much to contemplate, and we don't talk. I just strip off her clothes and make her hum with pleasure all the while thinking about that little pink case in her bathroom drawer that's almost empty.

# Chapter 27

## Cadence

**M**y sister's sleepy face on the screen of my phone makes me want to cry. Her long brown hair is draped over her face as she holds the phone at an angle so I can barely see her eyes.

"Good morning!" I sing into the speaker as she groans.

"Time differences, Cadence. It's 5:46am here."

I see my sister's husband walk by in his running shorts. "Morning, Alex."

He leans down so I can see his face on the screen. He's still as handsome as ever, but he doesn't have the rugged texture that Callum does, something I never thought I'd appreciate before. I haven't told Sunny about Callum yet, not really, and I've never kept a boyfriend from my sister. I literally tell her everything, but now how can I possibly tell her that I'm in a very happy, semi-committed relationship with a priest?

When I hear my brother-in-law leave the house, I yell

at Sunny to wake up and talk to me. As good as it is to see her, I'm not just calling for anything. I'm having a crisis. A real crisis.

"Sunny, wake up. I need you."

Her head peaks up and she stares at the camera with one eye open. Sisters can tell when someone is not right, and right now, her sensors are going off. "What's wrong?"

"I need something."

"Sure, yeah what is it?"

I take a heavy breath and I remind myself this is what sisters are for. We answer the call no matter what.

"I need you to send me some birth control." The moment the words are out of my mouth, Sunny's face goes blank for a moment before the disappointment sets in.

"Cadence," she drawls, dropping her head back down on the pillow.

"Listen, it's not what you think. I'm in an actual relationship." My cheeks burn from the width of my smile as I say those words out loud.

"You've been there for two months."

"Three, actually."

"Still!" My sister places the phone on the nightstand giving me a view of her ceiling while I hear her climb out of bed. I worry my lip as I wait for her to respond.

"Ireland has universal healthcare, Cadence. Go to the doctor there."

"What if they don't have the one I like? Can't you just get one of those fake scripts you used to get and send me some?" I know my voice is taking on a whiny tone, but I don't want to see a doctor here, and I don't know why. I still feel like an outsider, and while I know I do have rights to the system since I have my visa, there is something holding me back.

"You're staying, aren't you? Mom said she couldn't get you to come back." My sister finally picks up the phone and I see her face in the dim light. I forgot how cute my little Sunny is, with her freckled cheeks and austere eyes.

"So that's why she came?" I ask, sitting back on my bed. "I had my suspicions."

We don't talk for a moment as the sound of her coffee maker whirs in the background and she picks up their orange tabby, George. Then, she looks at me in the camera with a blank expression. "Who is he, Cadence?"

"Well, you're going to love this. He's a lot older than me. Older than Alex even."

"It is the priest then, isn't it?"

My stomach plummets. "Mom sure did tell you everything."

I'm not quite used to Sunny and Mom having this sort of open relationship. The two never got along when I was growing up. I was mediating between them constantly, up until the point that Sunny moved out and Mom quit drinking.

"Cadence!" Sunny's voice is tired sounding as she scolds me.

"I didn't call you to be lectured on the decisions I make with my own life."

"So what are you going to do? Be his mistress forever? How long can that possibly last? If he really loved you—"

"Don't say what you're about to say, Sunny. You don't even know him." I didn't expect our conversation to get so heated and emotional. I thought I could confide in my sister, spill my heart and let her feel how genuinely happy I am, but it's clear that judgement comes first here.

And I get that she's trying to protect me, but it's too late for that. I'm already long gone, so at this point, she might as well wave me off and wish me well because there is no coming back.

"I'm just calling it like I see it, Cadence. I want to be wrong, and I want to think that he's sleeping with you because he cares about you and not so he can have his cake and eat it too."

Tears fill my eyes. My sister feels like a traitor at the moment. She doesn't even know him. "I love him, Sunny." When I look up at her through my tear-soaked lashes, I see the pity in her expression and I want to scream. I am the girl who cried love one too many times. How could anyone believe me now?

Sunny puts George down and bites her lip as she stares at me. "I believe you, Cadence, but you called me asking for birth control when you can easily get it there. Maybe the reason you don't want to go to the doctor is because you don't really want the pill."

My face twists in confusion as I stare at her. "What are you talking about?"

"I'm talking about you constantly making decisions based on what other people want. I can see what you want, Cadence. You want a future with a man, a future *this man* can't have with you."

"I'm not trying to get pregnant, Sunny. That's insane."

"Someday, don't you want that?"

My throat is filled with needles as I swallow down the words she's saying—the long held truth, layered with the secret she's held for me for so long. She's digging up skeletons to serve me with the dose of reality I need. Yes, that is something I want someday, more than anything.

How long will I do this with Callum before my waiting becomes too much? If he can't give me what I want, then why am I torturing myself with it now?

"I'm sorry, Cadence. I hate to make you cry."

My beautiful, sweet Sunny. So blunt. So harsh, appropriately named for being a ray of sunshine that will literally burn you if you're not careful. She's also painfully wise, and I hate her for it. I hate that she fell in love with Alexander so confidently, never looking back, never second-guessing. I hate that I'm four years older, and I make every dumb decision in the book. I'll probably be married ten times without ever finding the real one, and maybe there is no real one for me.

It would be Callum, I know it. I could see myself growing old with him, making him laugh, pushing his buttons because I can. Arguing with him late into the evening and making up in only the best ways.

I find it laughably unfair how I've probably met the only right man for me, and I can't have him.

"I'm fine," I lie, wiping my tears and turning on a fake smile.

It doesn't do much to convince Sunny. "I won't let you go without the pill, so if you really don't want to go—"

"I'll go to the doctor," I say, interrupting her. "Don't worry about it. I need to just go anyway, so I'll do it."

"So you're really staying, huh?"

With a subtle grin, I nod. "I'm staying. For now. I'm working on a new social media plan for the B&B. We're getting ready for the fall break, and I hope to have the house full by next summer. Hey, we'll probably need an extra pair of hands around here." I wink at her, but she shakes her head with a frown.

"No thanks. I've done enough international travel for a while. The only thing I want to do is stay home."

It's still so hard to think of my sister married, and I can tell she's still uncomfortable even saying it. I won't be that way when I get married. I'll want to scream it from the rooftop, wearing that badge with pride.

*I found love. It's mine, and I'm keeping it.*

The thought makes me sad again, but I don't let Sunny see it. "Okay, I gotta get back to work. Sorry to wake you. Have a good day. I love you."

"Wait, Cadence." I pause and look back down at my phone. "You're stronger than you think."

She blows me a kiss a moment before the phone goes black. My sister's words echoed from the first time I called her ring through my mind. As I make my way back downstairs to help Bridget in the garden, I think about what my sister said.

Why am I dragging my feet about the doctor? Is it because I don't see myself staying in Ireland? Finding a doctor is definitely something a settled person does...not some long-term tourist.

Or am I holding off for another reason?

"What's on your mind?" Bridget asks as I rake up the leaves around the yard.

"Huh?" I pause and look up at her.

"You're about a million miles away right now." She laughs playfully.

"Oh, sorry. I didn't sleep much last night." As I shake my head and get back to work, I hear her almost silent scoff. My eyes glare up at her.

"What was that?" I ask.

"Come on, Cadence. It's not like you two are very subtle about it." When she looks up at me, my cheeks flush hot. His sister knows. My sister knows. This has only been really going on for a month and already too many people know.

"I—um, I don't—" I stammer, but she laughs again.

"Listen. I don't care what my brother does, and his vows are his vows. I've honestly never seen him so happy, but I'd be a little more careful if I were you."

"You're not mad?" My voice sounds so small.

"Why would I be mad? It's your life."

"I know, but Callum…"

"Always was a terrible priest." She sniggers. "I can't say I saw this coming though. Callum was always so focused on work and duty, that I worried he would miss his whole life. I always hoped something would change his mind…"

Something heavy lands at the pit of my stomach. "He's not changing his mind."

"What do you mean?"

It feels like my chest won't let me take deep breaths and I'm stuck sucking in short shallow ones. "I mean it's just sex."

Bridget flinches. I know being so flippant about sex isn't for everyone, but now I'm frustrated. Between this conversation and the one I just had with my sister, it feels like everyone on earth wants me to know what a stupid decision I'm making.

"Really?" Bridget asks.

"Yes. Now maybe you're not so supportive, huh? Callum and I are having sex, and he's still a priest, and he's going to stay a priest." I turn in a huff and start raking again, this time a little more aggressively.

She doesn't respond, but Bridget isn't a bold woman. She accepts my answer with an apologetic expression and gets back to her gardening. I feel her eyes glance up my way every few minutes, and it only grates on my nerves more.

At dinner, the tension is thick. Callum walks in from work with a pleasant expression, and he immediately reads the room, looking at both of us like he's missing something. There are guests in the parlor and an older couple joining us for supper.

We make small talk and I do my best to pretend that

everything is fine. They love talking to Callum like he's some feature of the hotel. *Dine with an authentic Irish priest.* Thankfully, I'm good at hiding my sour mood with fake smiles and engaging conversation.

When we turn in that night, I avoid Callum in the bathroom, stepping out just before he comes up the stairs. It's not that I'm not in the mood tonight. Actually, quite the opposite, but since I'm on my little white pill instead of the pink ones, I'm on my period. Not that I think he would care at this point, but my stupid cycle and those pills and that conversation just spike the anger in my mood reminding me that I am still a booty call. This is just sex. My life remains on hold.

The gentle tapping against my door after I crawl under my covers is expected. My room is dark, with only the light from the moon illuminating it.

"Come in," I whisper, and a moment later, it creaks open.

Feeling his presence makes my chest constrict. I want to scream, mostly because I agreed to this. I was part of this arrangement, and I have no one else to blame. He asked me if I would stay for him, and I agreed. Of course that was before we started doing what we're doing now.

But I'm still mad at him. I'm mad that he's going along with it, treating me like a piece of ass when I thought I meant more to him. I had myself convinced that he would change his mind and abandon the church for me. It was a stupid thing to think.

"What the bloody hell is going on?" he whispers after closing himself in.

I turn onto my side, facing him, but not moving to get up or welcome him into my bed. "I'm on my period." For some reason, I hope it turns him away or makes him leave, but of course, it doesn't.

"What's bothering you?" He steps closer. Instead of getting in my bed, he kneels on the floor next to it so that his face is not far away from mine. Seeing his tan skin in the moonlight makes me want to kiss him so badly.

I get choked up as I answer. "I just told you."

His callused hands stroke my hair away from my face with so much tenderness that it reminds me of the day I watched him hold that baby in the Christening. "Cadence," he says as a warning, and it's all it takes to break me. The way he reads me, knows when something is wrong and pushes for answers even when I don't want him to make something in me bend.

"What are we doing, Callum?"

When he hears the strain in my voice, he leans his head down so that his lips are against my cheek. "I thought this was what you wanted," he whispers.

"I thought so too, but how long can we do this? What if I wake up one day, and my whole life has passed me by?"

"We're taking it one day at a time," he moans.

There are so many things I want to tell him, things I've been holding back, afraid if he knew about them he would never truly love me. My lips fall silent when I have the chance.

When the quiet consumes us, he stands and moves toward the door. His distance starts to feel like actual pain, so I sit up in a rush. "Please don't leave."

I watch his shoulders rise and fall with a heavy sigh. Without another word, he turns around and pulls off his shirt, revealing his sculpted chest with the spatter of hair that leads down to his boxer shorts. Then, he climbs into bed next to me and lets me nuzzle my face against his chest.

He holds me all night, never moving to touch me for more. I think he's feeling the weight of this situation the same way I am. We didn't choose this, but we're stuck in it together.

I don't want to take his life from him.

He doesn't want to take mine from me.

But at the moment, we can't live without each other.

# Chapter 28

## Cadence

"Can I pet the horse?"

Bridget, Daisy, and I are cleaning out the garden bed when a family of four with two small girls with blonde pigtails come walking up to us. Looking up from under the brim of my hat, I smile.

"Of course you can." Dropping my trowel, I pull off my gloves and walk the girls over to where Misty is standing at the fence. I convinced Callum that we needed to open Misty's pen, letting her come closer to the house, that guests would love to see her, and it's been a hit. There are pictures of her with guests on our review sites already, shoving those *other* reviews farther down—the ones that talk about me.

"Her name is Misty," I tell the girls as the horse comes trotting closer. I have a few treats for her in my pocket that I drop in each girl's palms. The taller one holds her hand out fearlessly. I'd guess she's about twelve. The younger one stands timidly behind her while the parents snap pics from across the yard.

"Will she bite me?" the girl asks in an adorable little British accent.

"Nope. Here, let me show you." I hold out a treat for Misty which she takes gently from my hand.

"Will you help me?" the little one asks.

I smile at their parents who give their girls a little thumbs up. Standing next to the little one, I hold her hand in mine and move it closer to Misty's mouth. She licks up the treats and the girl giggles loudly, squirming with delight.

"It's so slobbery!"

They erupt in giggles and I quickly retrieve more food for them to feed the horse. Misty lets them pet her as I answer their questions, and I'm so distracted that I don't even hear the van pull up.

I'm in the middle of listening to Maisy, the seven-year-old, tell me all about her pet dog, Chupa, her pink bedroom, and her best friend from school when I look up to see Callum watching from the driveway. He's in his clerical attire with a couple of heavy boxes in his arms and that familiar smug expression that I remember from the first day I walked into this house.

After the girls take off with their parents, I walk into the house to greet him. He's sorting the mail at the kitchen counter.

"I told you bringing Misty closer would be great for business. She's so good with guests."

"So are you," he replies as he looks around cautiously before pulling me in for a quick kiss. I want to stay in his arms as he pins me against the counter with his hard body, but I pull away before any one of our guests can walk past.

The house has been full for weeks, and it's been working us all to the bone.

"This came for you," he says before handing me a bubble package with Sunny's handwriting on it. I go silent as it registers what my sister has sent me.

I snatch it out of his hands and feel the thick envelope, knowing exactly what's inside.

Callum watches me curiously like he's waiting for me to fill him in. I swallow and look away instead.

"Are you going to tell me what it is?"

I can feel the refill packs between the bubbles of the padded envelope. Of course, Sunny came through. Even when she knew I could make the appointment myself, she knew that I wouldn't. She came through because she wants me to be safe. She doesn't want what happened to me before to happen again.

What she doesn't know is that it wouldn't. I won't let it.

As I look up at Callum, the heaviness of our last conversation between us, I try to force a smile. This is good news. We're in the clear, and we don't need to buy condoms or keep our distance.

Clearing my throat, I rip open the package. I want him to know what it is. As I pull the round, silver refill packs out of the package, I hold them up.

"Hallelujah."

Callum doesn't smile. In fact, he looks contemplative as he takes it from my hand. For a moment, he considers them, and then his eyes meet mine. As he presses my body against the counter, he reaches around me to drop the package in the trash on the other side.

"What are you doing?" I jump to grab it but he twists me back so I'm facing him. His lips find mine and he kisses me fervently, his tongue invading my mouth and making me want to strip off my clothes right here.

*What is happening?* my mind screams.

"You really want to fish those out?" he whispers against my lips. My mouth hangs open as I stare at him. What the fuck is he saying? I'm trying to piece together everything I'm hearing, afraid that I'll jump to the wrong conclusion.

"Do you want me to?" I ask.

"No, I don't."

The air leaves my lungs, and I grip his shirt between my fists. I've forgotten about being secretive, other guests, Bridget, or anyone else, and I pull him closer.

"Callum," I gasp. Inside my chest, my heart has started to hammer away, filling my body with heat. This is one of those big moments, a turning point. But why would he do this? What is he saying?

For a moment, I dare to hope this is the moment he's about to tell me I'm his and he's mine, and a flutter of anxiety to my stomach suddenly makes me question how I feel about that. About all of this.

His hands reach up to hold my face as he kisses me again. "You didn't answer my question, Cadence. Do you want to fish them out?"

I can hardly breathe let alone answer. What Callum is asking me isn't something I can answer lightly. Do I want to take that risk? End up pregnant with his child, his baby. Even if we can never be public. Is that what I want?

My heart nearly explodes at the thought. Yes. Emphatically, yes. When he threw that package away, he wasn't taking my choice. He was answering the question I was too afraid to ask.

What if?

What if we could have everything we wanted?

I don't even care enough to understand what this all means about him and us and the future. What he's offering has me too excited to give a damn.

"No," I whisper. "No, I don't want them." My voice cracks on the words, and he kisses me again, but this time I kiss him back hungrily.

The front door opens and we break apart in a rush. He returns to sorting out the boxes he brought in, and I grab the junk mail from its pile and shove it into the trash, pushing Sunny's package far enough down that it won't be retrievable. Then I look at him with a smile.

He touches my chin before Bridget can turn back around.

Whatever the future holds I don't know. And people might think this is crazy, considering a child with a priest who can never marry me, never be truly ours, but Callum knows what he's giving me, that he's feeding a part of my soul in ways he doesn't even know.

Still, that nagging sense of doubt refuses to go away. This time, my life isn't the only one I'd be ruining. Am I making yet another mistake?

# Chapter 29

## Callum

Time feels like it's slipping past us. Every time I look at her, I wonder: how did this happen? When did everything change? When was the exact moment I fell in love with her?

She's sitting next to me in the car on the way to Dublin, and my pulse won't stop thrumming in my ears. Every moment or so, I glance over at her. She's staring out the window, much like she did when we made this drive three months ago. In her knee-length blue dress with the little white flowers and a plunging neckline, she looks so different from the girl who landed on my doorstep. She wears a new confidence she didn't have before, like she's no longer looking for validation. There's a new sense of pride in how she works at the house that's changed the way she carries herself now. And I can barely keep my hands off of her with how fucking sexy it makes her to me.

This is not a fling. It's not sex. Somewhere in the past

three months, this thing between us became everything. I would give it all up for her.

I plan to. I just haven't told her that yet.

She reaches across the seat and links her fingers with mine. Gently, I lift them to my lips and kiss each knuckle. I didn't tell her that I booked us one of the nicest hotels in my budget in Dublin. We are doing far more than picking up her paperwork from the consulate. She has no idea just how much, but she will soon.

The trip to the consulate is quick, and as we walk out of the building, she leans on my arm, our hands still grasped together.

"I love being able to hold your hand in public."

And I love it too. I like that people see us together, and I don't care that I look more like her dad than her boyfriend. Out here, she's mine and I don't need to hide.

I haven't given much thought to what happens after everything, if we'll still feel comfortable in Ennis, if everyone will give her a hard time because of a choice *I* made, but none of that matters. We'll find a way.

Turning her body toward me, I place my hands on her face. Then, I kiss her more than any man should kiss a woman in the middle of a busy street, let alone a priest. She doesn't stop me. She leans in. This will all be mine soon. Kissing her in public, being wholly and completely hers.

"I have a surprise for you," I whisper as she pulls away. Her eyes light up.

"Please tell me we don't have to hurry home. I want to stay like this for just one day."

My heart throbs hearing her say that. She deserves so much more than one day, and I can't fucking wait to give it to her. So I kiss her gently on the forehead and pull her down the road to the car.

After a short drive, we pull up to the hotel, dropping the car off at the valet. Cadence is biting back a smile as I open the lobby door for her, watching her expression as she walks through. Red flower sculptures hang from the ceiling with a white marble floor at our feet, and the woman behind the counter greets us with a pleasant smile. Cadence is practically vibrating in my arms as we check in.

When we get to our room, which is simple with a large bed, red velvet pillows propped on a deep gray duvet, Cadence falls onto it with a bounce. What I wouldn't pay to see this smile on her face everyday.

"I love this surprise." She beams.

I stand between her legs and crawl carefully over her body. "I figured you might."

She pulls my face down and kisses me deeply, her hands roaming my body, reaching for my belt buckle. I don't bother telling her that we have a lot planned for the day. For just one moment, she feels like mine. We are a regular couple, and this is our hotel room.

It doesn't take long before our kiss turns heated, and I trail my lips down her neck and over the deep neckline of her dress. Her moans are louder than normal, and I know she's thinking the same thing that I am. We've had to keep it down so much that it will feel so fucking good to make her really cry out. To hear her whimpers and screams without a care in the world for who else hears them. Right now, I want all of fucking Dublin to hear them.

"Let's see if we can get a noise complaint," I say as I drop to my knees between her legs. It's practically an attack on her sex as I devour her, my short stubble scratching her thighs. She writhes and moans all the same.

"Louder," I hum against her. She answers with a guttural cry and I nearly come in my pants.

With my tongue buried deep inside of her, I reach up

207

and shove her dress up to her neck so I can hold her breast in my hands. I want every inch of her. I want to ruin her for anyone else. I want to make sure she knows she's mine and no one else can please her like me. No one will ever get the chance.

She calls out my name as her orgasm wracks through her, her thighs seizing up around me, and I know she did that for me. Like she was claiming me at the same moment I was claiming her. Letting God know who I belong to.

As I stand up, I stare down at her, and I unbutton my pants, dropping them to the floor. With my hands under her legs, I yank her body to the edge of the bed and enter her in one fluid motion.

She barely has the chance to come down from her last climax before she's writhing again. Watching her beautiful body on the bed, her legs wrapped around me, my chest aches. I love her so fucking much it hurts.

Grabbing her hand, I pull her up, and without pulling out, I lift her body in my arms. She has a drunk, ecstasy-laced smile as I carry her to the bathroom counter. With the large mirror behind her, I see myself as I fuck her.

For the first time in a long time, the reflection doesn't repulse me. It feels right.

She notices me looking and turns her head to see what I see. "I want to watch too," she whispers, and without hesitation, I spin her around and enter her from behind. Our eyes meet in the mirror as I slam into her, and I see her fight the urge to close her eyes or look away. The intensity of staring at each other as we both careen toward this climax is the most spiritual experience I've ever felt.

My whole life I've been seeking out a connection with God, and I had no idea the transcendental power of connecting with another person.

Just before I come inside her, I grab her body and pull

it roughly against mine. She claws at my arms as her body tenses and tremors against mine. I feel her orgasm in my bones.

We both stand there panting a moment before I press my lips against her neck and whisper against her skin.

"I love you."

She doesn't even react, no gasp or flinching. She spins in my arms, kissing me as if she's kissing the words that just came out of my mouth.

"I love you too."

I want to come out with it right at that moment. The words are hanging on my lips, but we have a long day planned, and I want to savor every single moment. This moment belongs to our first 'I love yous'.

After we get cleaned up, we head back out into the city. I hold her hand every step of the way and when we sit at dinner that night, I have to hold back from kissing her when I should be eating. I'm addicted to this feeling of having her to myself. I want it forever.

# Chapter 30

## Cadence

Callum's hand rests at my lower back as we walk, and I love the way it feels there. Everything about this day has been a dream. Being able to hold his hand in public, have loud sex that earned us a glare from the hotel staff as we walked through the lobby, sitting with him at dinner and talking about anything that wasn't the house or the church. For one day, he feels like my real boyfriend.

I'm waiting for reality to come crashing down. Because what I seem to be living in is like some rose-colored daydream where Callum and I can create a future together regardless of rules and boundaries. We've established that we love each other, and we're doing literally nothing to prevent bringing a child into this relationship, but the harsh rules are still in place. We're not listening to them, we're just living despite them.

It's exhilarating, but at the same time, that nagging fear

that I'm making a terrible mistake won't let me fully relax into whatever this is.

The streets of Dublin are so much bigger, louder, and busier than Ennis. I feel like I could get swallowed up here, and I miss the comfort of the streets I'm used to, so I hold tight to Callum's side as we stroll past busy pubs and dimly lit restaurants. When we reach the river, he guides me to a long bridge that spans across, and we walk quietly toward the center, where we stop and he turns me. The moon reflects on the water, the streets of the city lit around it, and it's breathtaking.

Granted, it's not Ennis beach at sunset, but it's beautiful nonetheless.

Just as I pull out my phone to snap a pic, he wraps his arms around me from behind.

"Cadence."

I answer him with my head resting against his chest, and just as his lips close in on the skin of my ear, I swear I can hear what he's about to say before he utters the words.

"I'm quitting."

Needles prick the skin of my neck. Turning to face him, I search his features for a sign that this is real, not a joke. "Wha—"

"I want to marry you."

It slams into me like a train, these confessions. The words I want to hear more than anything come raining down without warning, and I try to breathe through the onslaught.

"Callum."

I can't breathe. My face is in his hands. Warm tears pool in my eyes as I drown in the intensity on his face. This is real. He's being serious, and I can't get time to slow down for one second long enough to let me catch up.

"What about the church?"

"It's not right of me to keep my vows to the clergy when they belong to you."

I squeeze my eyes shut, letting the tears fall. This is what I wanted. This is *everything* I wanted, and I'm overcome with it. I've never been happier in my entire life than when I'm with Callum, and I don't think I would ever tire of him. He makes me better in every way, and I think I do the same for him.

There should be absolutely no doubt in my mind that this is everything I want...but that nagging doubt refuses to be ignored.

Is this Clint all over again? If I give everything to Callum, will he change his mind? Will he break my heart when it's at its fullest? Especially when he learns everything.

"Marry me, Cadence."

I gasp again, squeezing his hands that are still cupping my face. It's like my dreams are staring me right in the face, and I can't work up the guts to reach out and take them. There are still things Callum doesn't know about me...things in my past that could be deal-breakers for him.

But with that look of love and hope in his eyes, I can't deny him. I can't force him to wake up from this dream when I know I don't want to.

"Yes," I answer through my tears, and his mouth is on mine, clutching my body to his so tightly I can barely breathe.

Once we break our kiss, everything feels different. We are both high on this new development, and the world feels like it's ours. Whatever problems we need to work out, we'll work them out later, together. Tonight, I want to enjoy this feeling.

. . .

The next morning as I wake up, I nuzzle myself against his body and kiss the center of his chest all the way up to his ear, and he groans as he starts to wake.

"What time is it?"

"Seven-thirty."

We were up well past one in the morning, trying to get that noise complaint we wanted so badly. When the phone did finally ring, we didn't answer it, but we did enjoy one last earth-shattering orgasm that shook the walls of our hotel room before we called it a night.

"We have to get back to the house," I say, peppering kisses along his neck and chest.

"Check-out isn't until eleven." His hands roam my body, and I feel him trying to tug my body on top of his.

"Callum, we have work to do."

"Look who's the responsible one now."

I don't protest as he positions me on top of him and fills me with a thrust. We do have a few minutes to spare, and as bad as I feel for leaving Bridget for a day and a half by herself, I can't turn down the way this feels with Callum because I know the moment we get back, everything will be different.

# Chapter 31

## Cadence

It's been three weeks since Dublin. It felt like a dream, and as soon as we got into the car to drive home, the dream ended and we woke up.

Callum said these things take time. He's working up his letter of resignation to his bishop, and I can see the stress it's causing him. He pours over the letter day and night.

We didn't tell anyone about his plan, and I feel the excitement of it all waning with every passing moment. At the dinner table, I see his eyes on me. I see the guilt he feels, the remorse for not doing what he promised he would, and I hate that this is tearing him up.

Reaching my foot across, I gently rest it against his leg, and I offer him a warm expression. It doesn't do anything to melt away the stress he's carrying, but I keep it there anyway.

As for me, I've managed to shelf my nagging doubts. For now.

Which is good because it's been replaced with a new form of anxiety. I'm two weeks late.

At first I figured it was just coming off the birth control that threw me off, but this morning, I noticed my breasts were sore and I could barely stomach the smell of sizzling ham from the kitchen.

Since buying a pregnancy test in a small town when you're the only American girl and word travels fast, I forego the physical evidence and accept it for what it is.

I'm pregnant.

It's not like I can be surprised about it. We've been banging like teenagers, and I haven't been on the pill in over a month. Still, I can barely get out of bed with the way my guilt is chewing at me.

How will I tell him? He has enough on his plate right now, but if he doesn't quit soon, people are going to do the math and realize that he and I were doing it long before he left his priesthood. What if he can't leave?

We really didn't plan this out. I know he'll be happy, or at the very least, he'll act happy. But I'll know that deep down...I'm just another responsibility for him. Between the farm and the church, he has to figure out what to do with his pregnant mistress, who is also his employee.

Callum's position at the church brings him income, albeit not a lot, it's still money, and if he quits, he'll be taking a pay cut. Can the hotel income support us all?

And then on top of everything, there's the constant reminder weighing on my soul that I have not been completely honest with Callum. And I wanted to tell him that before all of this happened, but we rushed it. We fucked up. *I* fucked up. Again.

Sick of soaking my pillow with my own pitiful tears, I climb out of bed and get dressed. I don't say a word to Bridget as I rush out the door. There's not an ounce of makeup on my face, and my hair is stacked messily on my head. I look as fucked up as I feel.

This needs to happen now. I can't wait another second, but the heavy emotion hanging on my heart nearly makes me want to turn around. Is bringing up the shitty things I've done in the past going to make anything right?

If Callum doesn't want me after he knows the truth, it's better to tell him now before it's too late.

He's in his office when I get to the church, and I storm in, slamming the door behind me. His head pops up from his Bible, and I notice he's writing his homily for tomorrow night's service—not his resignation letter.

"Cadence." His brow is furrowed, like he's angry, and I watch it morph into concern as he takes in my appearance.

"I have to tell you something." My voice cracks.

"Sit down," he commands, but I can't. I'm buzzing with energy, and I know if I sit, it will fizzle out and I'll change my mind.

"No. I did something, and you have to know about it because you may not want me anymore once you know." A sob shakes through my body, but I bite it back. He stands up, and I want to melt into his arms. I crave the comfort of his touch, but I can't have that right now. I need to do this first.

Carefully, I take a long, steady inhale. Then I let the words out. "When I was sixteen, I got pregnant."

That word alone stings. The memory is tied to it, and it immediately triggers painful memories I've never been able to bury.

He doesn't answer, but he searches my features, waiting for me to continue.

"I wanted to keep it," I sob, nearly doubling over from the pain, remembering how badly I hurt. "But my parents…"

Callum reaches for me, but I snatch my body away. Quickly, I say the next part before I chicken out. "I didn't. I didn't keep it, Callum. I had an abortion."

He flinches, and I catch it. I watch the way he changes when he learns this about me. Hot tears leak across my cheeks as I clutch my abdomen, knowing what it hides. Feeling as if this is all too much, and I've somehow managed to fuck up so royally, I will never recover.

"Why are you so upset?" He reaches for me again, but I back myself against the door.

"Because that should be a deal-breaker for you. Because you have values that make you better than me, Callum, but you overlook them all the time."

"What are you talking about?" His voice has deepened, growing frustrated.

"You're Callum, the rule follower," I sob. "That's what you do. You follow the rules, do your duty, live your life guided by something or *someone* else, and now you're letting me determine your life, but you need to know the truth about me."

"I do know the truth about you," he says so loudly it shakes the painting on the wall. Things are spiraling, and I see the panic set in his eyes. He's starting to feel helpless because I'm tearing myself away, crumbling the walls of the sacred place we built together, and there's nothing he can do to stop it.

"Cadence, I don't care about what you did when you were sixteen. If you think my values make me better than you, then you don't know me at all."

"I know you'll do what's expected of you. You live for your duty, and I know I came into this town as a temptation. I seduced you and as soon as you started fucking me, you realized that you'd have to do the right thing. You'd have to marry me."

"Stop it," he snarls with piercing anger in his eyes.

Every part of my body aches. This emotional pain is physical, and I hate myself for coming here and starting this, but I have no choice. I'm finally doing the right thing when for so long I've been doing nothing but fucking up.

"Tell me I'm wrong, Callum. I know it eats you up that you've been sleeping with me without being married to me."

"Why are you doing this?" His fists are clenched at his side.

"Why haven't you turned in that resignation letter?" I cry, pointing at the open laptop on his desk.

"I told you—"

"These things take time, I know. But I don't think you want to resign, Callum. I think you're torn. Torn by duty, torn because you don't know who to follow anymore, God or me."

"Just because I'm torn doesn't mean…"

"I don't want to tear you away anymore." Nausea bubbles up my chest as I watch his anger melt away. It hurts so much, but I have to do this. It's bad enough I've ruined my life; I don't need to ruin his life too. If I stay, he'll leave the church, work himself to the bone at the house. And there's no going back from that. I love him too much to watch his devotion to me ruin his life.

"Don't do this." His cold-faced plea nearly breaks me.

"I'm going home, Callum."

When he doesn't move, his eyes still focused on my face, I bite down my guilt and send one last shot, putting this beautiful daydream out of its misery.

"Home, home. I'm going back to Pineridge."

# Chapter 32

## Callum

I have lived my life at God's will. It was His will that led me to my ministry. For twelve years, I served Him without fault.

So why has He brought me to this? Why has He shown me love, given me the keys to a different life, if only to take them away?

If this is providence, faith in His plan, then my faith is failing.

"Are you sure about this?" Bishop Hawthorne asks in his office. My letter sits on his desk, and I'm across from him, my hands shaking in my lap.

"I am."

He leans back, seemingly in thought. He begins to drone on about commitment and God, advising me to pray on it longer and what verses to read before I decide to go through with this, but I've tuned him out. I nod along, and persist when he asks me again.

I'm really doing this.

Cadence boarded her plane last week. Bridget and Daisy sobbed all morning, and neither of them spoke to me when they came home from the airport. I can't be in the house, but I can't be in the rectory either.

Everything that happened that day came down so fast, but I'd be lying if I said I didn't expect it. We rushed things that were too delicate to be rushed. We brushed aside the conversations that we were both afraid would end what we had built, but I know that if we had faced them when we were supposed to, it might not have ended like this.

She was right. I was going to marry her out of duty. What kind of man would I be if I didn't? But she didn't put the faith in me, in us, that I needed. Those doubts and fears I watched swirl around her head tore us apart, and all I could do was revise my fucking letter one more goddamn time.

I should have turned this in three months ago. My ass should have been in this chair the first time I watched her lips move, hanging on every word like it was God who spoke them. I was a coward.

I asked her to hang around for me. I kept her hidden like a dirty secret and then somehow acted surprised when everything imploded. Of course she doubted my loyalty.

But the moment she walked out that door, I promised myself I would not contact her again until I was available in the way she deserves. Unfortunately, my line about these things taking time wasn't a lie. To become laicized can take up to a year or more, which is why I'm here to beg Bishop Hawthorne for mercy and to get this process rolling faster than usual.

Without sounding too disrespectful.

"I can't convince you to stay through Christmas, can I?"

"I'm sorry."

It's already September. I hate to think about the holi-days without Cadence. The sooner I get this over with and get her back, the better. If it's not already too late by then.

# Chapter 33

## Cadence

The weather this time of year is perfect. I'd be enjoying it a lot more if I could leave my bed. Luckily for me, Sunny and Alexander have a beautiful pool house equipped for guests that gives me enough sunshine through the floor-to-ceiling windows that I don't have to feel bad about my lack of vitamin D.

When I hear Sunny come through the door, I try to pretend to be asleep but she knows me better. I feel her settle onto the bed behind me, cuddling close so that her arms are wrapped around my waist. Then she nuzzles her face into my hair.

I didn't realize how much I missed my little sister until I spotted her as I came out of the terminal into the airport. I thought I had cried out every last tear I had until my eyes found little Sunny standing alone behind the rope waiting for me. I couldn't stop the tears as I ran into her arms and sobbed onto her shoulder.

Since then, I've answered questions vaguely, but when

your sister runs off to Europe, falls in love with a priest, and comes home knocked-up, it's not exactly a mystery as to why she's so upset. So she's been giving me my space.

But now that I've been home for a couple weeks, I can feel her getting restless and ready to talk.

"How are you feeling?" she asks, and I know she means physically.

"Tired. Sick. Sad. The trifecta."

She squeezes me tighter. "Do you know how far along you are?" It's the first time she's really asked about the pregnancy since I got here, and I want to push away the thought. So I just shrug.

"I don't know. A month. Maybe six weeks?"

Moving slowly to keep the room from spinning on me and sending me to the bathroom, I sit up and face my sister cross-legged. She does the same, and soon I'm reminded of all the years she and I sat on our beds like this, talking about boys. Well, it was usually me talking about boys while Sunny listened, never judging. It was like she looked up to me then, and I'm so glad she didn't follow in my footsteps. She found the one guy for her and she's perfectly happy spending her whole life with him, but that's always how Sunny was. She knew what she liked, what she wanted, and she went out and got it.

I see her sad expression as she watches me, and I know what she's thinking. Sunny was just a kid when I got "in trouble" as Mom refers to it. I remember that day so vividly, how mad Dad was, complaining about how much it would cost him and blaming Mom because she didn't watch me enough.

No one asked me what I wanted, but what choice did I have? I couldn't do it without them, so I had to do what they wanted. And I did. My life was expected to return to normal after that, and all I wanted was to find a man who wanted me, who would give me what was taken away so long ago, to right past wrongs.

Looking up at my sister, I clutch my stomach. Needles burn the backs of my eyes as she bites her lip, and I already know what she wants to say.

"Don't ask me what I'm going to do, okay?"

"I wasn't," she answers as moisture pools around her blue irises.

"Because I know what I have to do."

She blinks a tear down her cheek. "I know you do."

My lip trembles. "I'm keeping it, Sunny."

"I know you are." Her hand jets out to grab mine and we squeeze each other impossibly tight. After a moment, my head drops down to her lap and I let warm tears fall. Her hand stroked my hair out of my face and across her legs.

"I hate to be the devil's advocate here," she adds after a few minutes. Oh, Sunny. Always the practical one. I know exactly where she's going with this one. "He deserves to know, Cadence."

I let out a groan. "I know he does, but you don't understand. He'll leave everything for me. He'll quit the priesthood, his family's business, fuck, I think he'd leave Ireland for me if he knew."

My sister's hand stops moving. Then in a sarcastic, low drawl, she adds, "Oh no, not a man who would give up everything for you."

Sitting up quickly, I dry my tears. "But that's the thing. He wouldn't be doing it for me. He'd be doing it because he thinks he has to."

Sunny's head tilts and her brow furrows. "Oh my God, Cadence. What did they do to you?"

"Who?"

Reaching out to stroke my hair, she says, "All the boys

who somehow collectively convinced you that no one could truly love you."

My shoulders slump, and I let out a heavy exhale. "Oh. That was me. I did that."

Later that day, I actually gather the strength to get out of bed, put on real clothes and join my sister and brother-in-law for dinner. It was a mistake.

Seeing them together, how in-sync they are, itching to constantly touch each other but choosing not to for my sake only makes me feel worse. It makes me miss him so much I have to excuse myself and go back to the pool house. I can't live like this, not forever. I have a tiny person on the way, and it's going to be up to me to take care of them.

Instead of going back to bed, I settle myself on the edge of the pool and dangle my feet in the water. Just behind Sunny's new house is our old house. Mom sold it after she got cleaned up, but the memories it held are still there. Memories of a young, naive woman who gave everything away too easily.

I think about what would have happened if I'd met Callum sooner. He would have been even more annoyed with me when I was younger. If we hadn't been forced together, I probably would have never given him a chance. He was too cold, too stern, and no fun.

Would he have brought me closer to God then? Am I any closer to Him now? I always figured I was at war with God, trying to steal someone who had pledged his faith to Him.

Regardless, I close my eyes, let my head hang forward, and I pray.

First, I pray for this baby.

225

Then, I pray for guidance so I don't fuck this up.

Last, I pray for Callum, and I ask God to keep him. Keep his faith, and if providence is real, then I want God to let Callum decide. Let him live his own life without feeling like he owes anyone anything. He doesn't belong to me, or to Bridget, or to God even.

What my sister said was true. I have to tell Callum about the baby, but first I want to know that I can do this alone if I have to. I don't want Callum thinking he has to take care of us. It'll take me some time to get things worked out, but for the first time in my life, I have faith in myself.

# Chapter 34

## Cadence

Three months later…

"Merry Christmas," I call to the housekeeping staff as I drop three boxes of home-baked cookies on the table in the break-room.

The three older women all answer with wide smiles and come running toward me with hugs and pats on my belly. It's still a bump small enough to be hidden by my uniform, but they love to rub it anyway. I know most pregnant ladies hate it, but I love it. The only reason they even found out I was expecting was because I couldn't stop rubbing it myself.

"Where are you headed looking so pretty?" Gertie asks as she touches my curled hair and dangling earrings.

"Midnight Mass, actually."

They all practically start glowing at that. I haven't told them about the baby's father, but I bet they wouldn't be as smitten with me if they knew the truth. Giving them all one last hug, I grab my bag with my uniform stashed in it, and head out the door.

I started at the Pineridge Inn three months ago, and I did not tell them about my situation. They gave me a good shift at the front desk, which was a blessing for someone with little experience and no education. My online classes don't start until January, but I'm hoping to move my way up and get at least one promotion by the time the baby comes.

The job is perfect, but it does make me miss the B&B most days. I still get to talk to guests, but no one wants to stick around and talk to the front desk girl the way they wanted to in Ennis. There are no sit-down dinners, and our continental breakfast isn't nearly as social. Still, it's great. I like the people I work with, and there's a certain satisfaction I get from getting each of our guests whatever they need.

I haven't talked to Callum yet, but I'm working up to it. There's a part of me that knows that when I do finally reach out to him, he's going to hate me for keeping this from him. Maybe that's why I'm waiting. So that he'll be so mad at me, he won't feel obligated to stay with me.

When I went to the doctor for the first time, and I heard that little heartbeat, I broke down and sobbed right there on the table. I heard Callum in that heartbeat, and I couldn't leave my bed for three days with how bad I felt about it. He's going to hate me for having to miss that, and I don't blame him.

Now I'm nearly twenty weeks, halfway there. I'm not as sick anymore, not as tired, but my hourglass has lost its shape, and I'm starting to look more like a potato than a person. Standing in heels at work has lost its appeal, so now I switch to a pair of Sunny's sneakers that I stole to get me through the day. I didn't expect pregnancy to move so fast.

Every night after I get off, I take this walk along the quiet downtown street, past the field of cherry trees to the church at the end of the road. The walks remind me of Ennis, and although California is nothing like Ireland, there are moments where I feel at home.

I haven't gone through conversion or anything like I'm supposed to join the faith properly, but when I first discovered the church after I started at the inn, I couldn't help but go in. It felt like he was there. He being Callum, and He being God. Like my heart had melted them into one, and I could be alone with both of them. It was the first time I felt the peace that I left behind, and I became addicted to it.

So I started going to Mass, skipping the Eucharist after I learned that Callum should have never let me receive it in the first place because it was strictly for actual Catholics. But then again, Callum shouldn't have done a lot of things we did.

In fact, Mass was the only thing that could really get me out of my funk. Not even work could do that. Once I started coming here, getting lost in the rhythmic cadence of the Hail Mary prayers, watching babies get christened and choirs sing, I felt like myself again.

I even made a few friends. Turns out there is a whole group of single Catholic women that meet once a week, and even though I told them I wasn't technically a member, they let me come anyway. In the church, we talk about being a woman and our relationship with God. Outside of the church, we talk about being a woman and our relationship with men. They're some of the funniest,

Sara Cate

dirtiest, most caring women I've ever met. And they all think I should call Callum.

I spot them waiting for me in front of the church, and I wave as I cross the street. Then a dark figure standing by the door makes me stop in my tracks. Standing in the middle of the street, I figure I must be seeing things. As he steps toward me, into the light, I start to feel lightheaded.

"Get your arse out of the street," he bellows, and his voice, that accent, knocks the air out of my lungs.

It does nothing to break me out of my daze, but the blaring car horn does.

Suddenly, he has my arm in a tight grip and he's dragging me to the curb at the bottom of the church steps.

"Are you okay?" he asks, and I stare up at him in awe. The streetlight behind him illuminates the golden hue to his hair which has grown a bit longer with the same gray strands along the crown and temple. But that's not the first thing my senses register. The first thing is his smell. It's the only way I know I'm not crazy and he's truly here. He has that same cologne and cotton smell, no longer with that acidic scent of cigarettes or the soothing smell of the anointing oils he used to carry.

"Callum," I say in one quick breath.

"Cadence, are you okay?" one of the girls calls out toward me in concern.

I glance toward my waiting friends, and the other ladies point toward Callum while mouthing, *Is that him?*

Quickly, I nod and wave toward them. "Go inside, ladies. I'll meet you in there."

As soon as they're gone, I turn toward Callum, holding my bag in front of me as if he would notice the tiny swell to my stomach. "What are you doing here?"

"Sunny told me you'd be here."

"In Pineridge, Callum. What are you doing in Pineridge?"

He doesn't answer, just tilts his head toward me, giving me that same same stoic, quiet expression I remember from my first days in Ireland, and it has me feeling weak. I could give into him at this very moment and forget about everything—well almost everything.

I have to tell him about the baby now, before he can say another word.

"Callum—"

"Can I take you to Mass? Then we can talk later?" He puts out his arm toward me, inviting me to take it, and I feel myself trembling as I touch the thick sweater that hugs his broad shoulders.

Without another word, he walks me inside. This church is about twelve times bigger than his in Ennis. There's a line at the door as we collect the programs from the usher. I walk him to where I usually sit toward the back. He sits down quietly next to me, and I look up at him, our eyes meeting for one charged moment.

Three months feels like years when you're missing someone so much everyday, but then when they're sitting right next to you, it's like there was never a moment apart.

As the service starts, I try to relax like I usually do. The music, the prayers, the warmth, and the smells, I try to lose myself in it, but Callum is sitting next to me, and I can barely breathe.

Then I glance at his face, and watch him as he prays, eyes closed and serious, and it's so beautiful, I feel myself getting misty-eyed. I try to tear my eyes away, but he is a force and I'm drawn in, unable to move. His eyes open and he turns toward me just as a tear falls from my face. He moves to catch it, and then I'm in his arms, sitting in the back row of this crowded service, but I don't care. He holds my body, and I weep silently against this chest.

Suddenly, he has me by the hand, pulling me toward the exit. Just through the doors, he turns and places my back at the wall. We can still hear the service going on behind us, and I'm desperate to keep his body away from mine so he doesn't feel the way it's changed.

"Cadence, you were right about everything," he whispers. "It was wrong of me to keep my vows while falling in love with you. You deserved better."

"Callum," I mumble trying to push him away, but he only presses closer.

"I should have never proposed to you until I was laicized."

"Wait." I look up at him with wide eyes. "It's Christmas...you should be..."

"I'm not a priest anymore, Cadence."

Just then, they begin a song behind us, and my ears are still ringing from his words. "What did you say?"

"I'm sorry it took so long. I promised myself I wouldn't talk to you again until I was a free man, and now I am. I'm yours."

"No, no, no." I snake my way out and rush through the door into the cold, night air. He calls after me, but I keep up my pace toward the hotel where my car is parked.

"I thought you'd be happy," he says, coming up quickly behind me. Then his hand is around my waist, across my bulging stomach as he pulls me back toward his body, and I feel him tense. I try to maneuver out of his grasp, but he feels it. I know he does.

"Cadence." There's that deep timbre that sends chills down my spine.

All of the words I've been sleeping with the last three months start spilling out of my mouth. "I am happy,

Callum. I'm sorry I left. I'm sorry I got scared, but I was afraid that you'd give up everything for me just because it was your duty, and I didn't know if I could ever accept that you really loved me."

His eyes are on my stomach, and I don't bother hiding it anymore. "Are you…"

"I'm sorry," I sob, dropping my hands into my face. "I should have told you sooner, but—"

His hand is around the back of my neck and I'm slammed against his chest as his arms engulf me. This time I let my stomach rest against his, and I feel his chest shudder as I do. We stand there for a while, listening only to the distant music inside the church and the sound of each other's breath.

Before pulling apart, his deep voice against my head sends chills down my spine. "Don't apologize to me again, Cadence. I'm the last person who deserves your confessions. I did give up my job for you, but I'd do it again and again because you're worth it. Don't ever doubt that again."

I pull my face away from his chest and our mouths crash together, his tongue against mine making me feel like I'm already home. His hands roam my body like he's remembering every old curve and learning every new one.

With his hands on my hips, he pulls his mouth away from me. "I want to see it."

And I know he means my belly, so I loosen my cardigan and open it so he can see the subtle rise and fall under my tight shirt. His fingers reach out and rub the gentle mound, and my throat begins to ache with the lump building there.

Then, right there on the street in front of the church, Callum drops to his knees in front of me. His hands still on my hips, he pulls my body until my stomach is against his lips. I stroke the thick hair on his head as I watch the toughest man I've ever known crumble.

I think I always knew he'd come, and maybe that's what I was waiting for. I always wanted Callum to make the first move. I needed to know he wanted me for me, and he crossed an ocean for me. These past three months were painful, but I needed him to make that step, and he needed me to stand up for myself. The months were hard, but our faith was stronger.

"Callum," I whisper. When he looks up at me with his red-rimmed eyes, I smile. "I want to go home."

# EPILOGUE

## Cadence

What a sight we are. An ex-priest standing at the front of the church while his very pregnant fiancé waddles her way down the aisle in all white. My dad couldn't make the trip on such late notice, but I wasn't going to let him give me away anyway. I want to walk myself down the aisle. Just me and this baby who could make his appearance any day now.

Sunny and Alexander and my mother all made it. And all things considered, Callum's congregation has been surprisingly supportive. Turns out they weren't much surprised when they heard the news. When I flew back to Ireland with him on New Year's Day, I expected an angry mob to meet me at the airport, cursing my name for driving their precious priest away.

But I should have known better. Every single person in town, with the exception of some jealous housewives, welcomed me back with open arms. They were too

235

distracted by the news of a wedding and a baby and a promise from Callum that he would still attend every Bible study and charity breakfast.

The walk down the aisle is a lot longer than I expected, but with the way Callum looks in this dusty, stained-glass sunshine, I could stand here forever. It still seems crazy to me that the person who truly sees me better than anyone was a priest. If you had told me this a year ago, I would have thought you were crazy, but it turns out that being a wild woman in search of validation and love in all the wrong places has a lot of parallels to being a holy man. Callum looked to God for love and validation, but for so many years of his life he missed the opportunity to connect with another person. We were both so lost.

But we're not anymore.

He's wearing that serious expression as I reach the altar, regardless of the fact that my face is desperately trying to split in two from my smile. He reaches out to take my hands just as Father Markus, the priest Callum convinced to take his place in Ennis starts speaking. The service drags on, and I don't hear a word. I'm lost in his eyes, trying to remember the first time I realized I loved him. I wish I could go back to that moment and tell myself then how this would end, just to see my expression.

When Father Markus finally pronounces us married, I don't feel any different. Maybe because the things we've done in this church, like the first time we did it on the floor of this very aisle, made us more bonded in the eyes of God than this wedding. That moment was a holy union, and it was even presided over by a priest.

After the wedding, we head to Yeager's for the reception. Everyone except for me and my mom proceed to get sloppy-faced drunk, even my new husband who won't take his hands off me for one second all night.

"Well, this is appropriate," I tease him. "On the day we met, you carried me home when I was drunk."

"Yeah, but I didn't take advantage of you like the way you're about to take advantage of me." I love the drunken drawl to his accent, the accent that still makes my toes curl. I lean in and plant my lips on his, and I take a deep inhale, absorbing that scent of his.

"That is true."

Under the table, I feel his hand work its way up my dress until it reaches the wedding night surprise I have for him. When he finds that there are no underwear there, he lets out a groan and tries to take a bite out of my shoulder. I'm glad my big ass stomach doesn't weird him out because I've never been hornier in my life. And that's saying something.

"Let's get out of here," I whisper, turning to say goodbye to everyone in the pub. A dull, throbbing pain in my back and hips slow me down as I try to stand. These pub seats were not made for pregnant women. I barely make it two steps before I realize that walking only makes it worse. Trying not to alarm anyone, I make polite small talk with a couple at the bar before trying to walk again.

Callum, even though he's drunker than a skunk, picks up on my weird behavior and the way I'm holding my back at a weird angle. In a heartbeat, he puts on a sober face and comes to my side.

"Please tell me your back is just sore."

"Umm...my back is really, really sore. I think this is it."

"Oh Jesus," he replies as his eyes widen. "But we're all drunk!"

"I'm not," my mother says from her seat at the table next to us. She stands up and places her hand on my stomach. "Oh yeah, that's a contraction."

It's like everyone in the pub hears her and the room

goes silent. Turning toward Callum with his serious expression and stern jaw, I let out a laugh. He's never looked more terrified, so I reach up and put my hands on his cheeks. "Can I get a raincheck on the honeymoon suite?"

As he pulls me in for a kiss, everyone in the pub lets out a howl of applause.

We probably should have had more than half a reception before we started having babies, but if I've learned anything this year, it's that I don't question God's plan. Sometimes we have to take the long road to get to where we're meant to be—a very long, very bumpy road.

\* \* \*

# Callum

Three years later…

"We have to hurry before he comes back," I whisper as I trail kisses down my wife's body, over her swollen breasts and across her soft belly which has carried not one, but two of my boys. She has on the blue dress I love with the deep neckline and white flowers, the one she keeps for this occasion alone, when Father Markus goes to the pub and leaves the church unattended for a couple hours.

With her hidden in the confessional, I sit on my knees in front of her, lifting her dress and watching her squirm with anticipation. I don't stop until I find the place where I know I would spend my day if I could. She lets out that familiar purr as my tongue parts her lips and plunges deep. I know that shit drives her crazy, as if the death grip she has on my hair could let me forget.

Just as I zero in on her clit with the right amount of suction, I slide in two digits and smile at the way she nearly levitates off the seat. How I went twelve years of my life without doing this, I don't know.

When I look back on my years as a priest now, it feels like that time of my life was my time in waiting. I don't regret it. I mean how could I? If I hadn't spent that time devoted to God and the service of others, I would have never been the kind of man Cadence deserves. I'm glad she didn't know me in my twenties. I wasn't right for her then, and it doesn't matter now that I'm pushing fifty and my life feels like it's just starting. I've never felt younger. I mean...look at how I get to spend my Saturdays.

"Callum," she gasps. She says my name every time I get my lips on her pussy. It's a tradition and her gift to me. With a little more pressure, I anticipate the moment her body seizes and she explodes with pleasure.

She doesn't waste any time and barely gives herself a chance to recover before she's reaching for me. And who am I to deny her what she wants?

I pull her out of the confessional and carry her to the office that used to be mine. She attacks my lips with her mouth, tasting herself there, and I can't move fast enough to get the damn pants undone as I place her on the soft chaise lounge. She helps me with the belt and as soon as my cock is free, she climbs onto my lap, straddling my hips and rides me like a horse.

It doesn't matter that we're the only people in the building or that I'm not a priest anymore. We still muffle our cries and pretend this is our dirty little secret.

Cadence loves to share our story, especially to the guests. Since Bridget got remarried and moved out with Daisy, Cadence made the B&B her own. Every single change she's put in place has only helped the business flourish. We've added riding lessons with Misty and brought on an actual staff. Even with two small kids, she never looks overwhelmed. In fact, she looks perfectly satisfied with the chaos of our lives.

Of course, finding alone time with kids and a business isn't easy, so when Father Markus asks us to volunteer at the church, we never pass it up. Because it means moments like this, her riding my cock in my old office while that bronze statuette of the Virgin Mary watches with disapproval.

When I feel her body tremble and shake, I take control and flip her onto her back. Taking her hands above her head, I growl in her ear.

"You've been a bad girl."

She squirms, biting back her smile. "Forgive me, Father," she moans in reply.

I don't know how I ever got so lucky, finding this beautiful girl. God was no match for Cadence, and if loving her was ever a sin, then I would gladly burn.

Slamming into her again, I come hard. She latches onto my body with her legs, squeezing me in place so I can't pull out.

"We have to lay here for a second. I don't want it to all come out."

"You're crazy, you know. Gabriel is only three and Noah's barely a year. Are you sure you're ready for another?"

She responds with a smile, her cheeks red and her lips swollen. It's a far cry from the girl who landed on my doorstep almost five years ago, lost and alone. She's anything but now. I know God meant for her to fall into my arms that day. I know He brought us together with intention, and maybe our method was a little unorthodox, and some might call it a scandal, but I still hold onto my faith in providence. Our love is not a sin; it's salvation.

* * *

*Oh Holy Night.*

Download the bonus epilogue and see Callum & Cadence on Christmas Eve a few years in the future…

www.saracatebooks.com

**Thank you for reading *Beautiful Sinner*.**

This was a scary book to write. There was so much I wanted to get right, but I also wanted to create a world where love was inevitable, no matter what it had to overcome. Yes, there is heat and sex, but at the core of everything I write, there is love. **Unbeatable, unstoppable, fearless, profound love**. That is what I hope I conveyed in this story.

If you loved Cadence and Callum, please consider leaving your opinion for future readers to see.

There should really be a lot of names featured on the cover of this book because I could not do it alone.

First and foremost, my sincere gratitude goes out to Adrian, who held my hand through the scariest writing I've ever committed to. Remember when I pitched this idea? You were scared, but you were a trooper. Thanks for sticking it out and for taking it rough. ;)

My beta readers: Suzanne and Susan—true VIPs.

My GLORIOUS assistant: Lori Alexander. Couldn't do it without you. You have no idea.

My dear friend, Rachel Leigh, for listening to every single idea. You're a saint.

My editor: Beth Hale of Magnolia Author Services

My cover designer: Barb Hoeter of Coverinked Designs

My graphic design artist: Amanda Shepard of Shepard Originals

And last but not least, the BEAUTIFUL members of Sara's Sweets, who are too many to name. Every day, I log in to that group because you lift me up. Thank you.

*muah*

# Also by Sara Cate

**Salacious Players' Club**

Praise

Eyes on Me

Give Me More

Mercy

**Wilde Boys duet**

Gravity

Freefall

**Age-gap romance**

Beautiful Monster

Beautiful Sinner

**Reverse Age Gap romance**

Burn for Me

**Black Heart Duet**

Four

Five

**Cocky Hero Club**

Handsome Devil

**Wicked Hearts Series**

Delicate

Dangerous

Defiant

# About Sara Cate

Sara Cate writes forbidden romance with lots of angst, a little age gap, and heaps of steam. Living in Arizona with her husband and kids, Sara spends most of her time reading, writing, or baking.

You can find more information about her at
www.saracatebooks.com